Ciscoe's Dance

(Dance & Listen Series Book 1)

Marion Hill

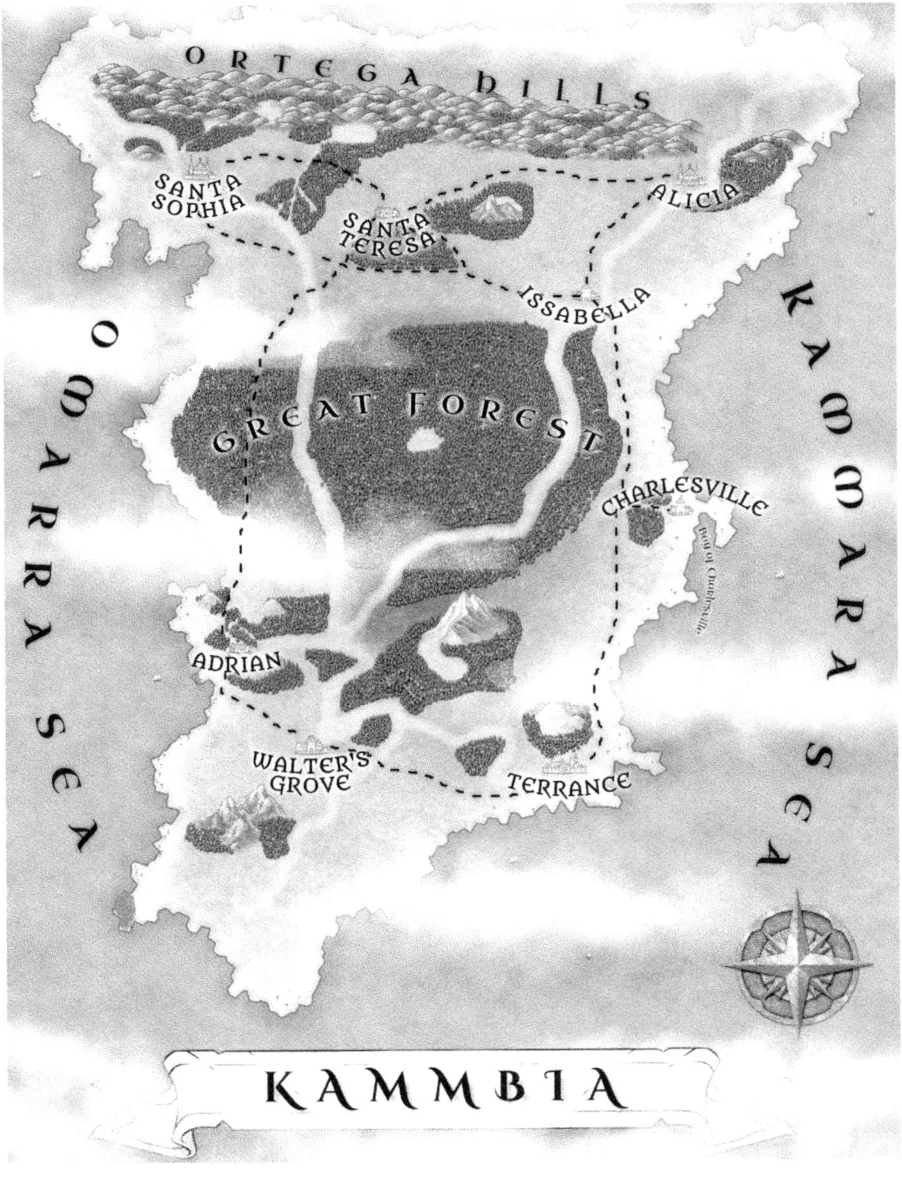

ORTEGA HILLS
SANTA SOPHIA
SANTA TERESA
ALICIA
ISSABELLA
KAMMARA SEA
GREAT FOREST
CHARLESVILLE
Bay of Charlesville
KAMMARA SEA
ADRIAN
WALTER'S GROVE
TERRANCE
KAMMBIA

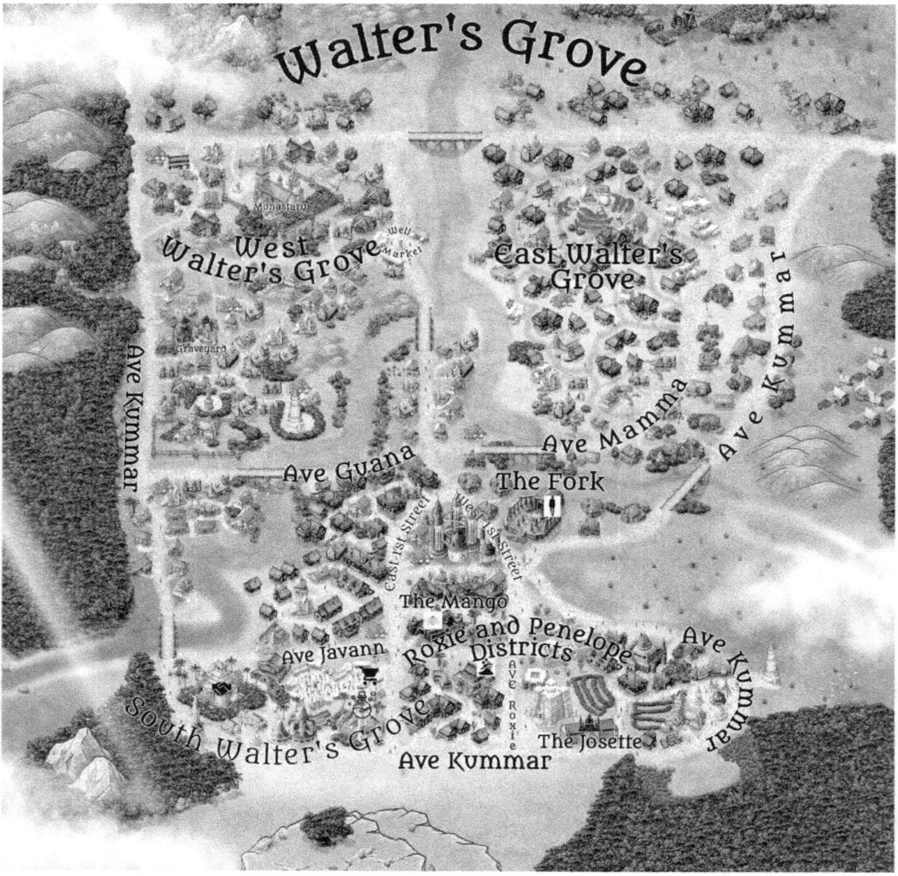

Walter's Grove
Monastery
West Walter's Grove
Well Market
East Walter's Grove
Graveyard
Ave Kummar
Ave Kummar
Ave Mamma
Ave Guana
The Fork
East 1st Street
West 1st Street
The Mango
Roxie and Penelope Districts
Ave Roxie
Ave Javann
Ave Kummar
South Walter's Grove
The Josette
Ave Kummar

Chapter 1

The line formed outside of the Mango Nightclub was nearly a full block as dusk arrived. The club was getting ready to open and the crowd outside seemed larger than usual for a midweek night. Antonio had not announced if there was another event happening tonight. I assumed that more people than usual wanted to hang out at one of the largest nightclubs in the Roxie and Penelope District.

A staff member escorted us to our designated section of the nightclub. Antonio gave us a private area to the left of the main dance floor. Latisha and I got dressed in our dannza outfits. I had on my black jumpsuit with silver on the sleeve and pant legs. My wife wore a silver knee-length dress with black trim at the bottom. As dannzas, we always wore our customary black and silver outfits when we performed at the Mango.

Patrons entered the nightclub a few minutes later and I heard Gerardo Torres' song, *Move, Move, Move* playing on the sound system. That song had become one of the standards for Piccanta music, which had taken over the city in the last several years. The musician Raphael Reynolds began promoting this new style of music about five years before and declared that Guanamamma music, started by Walter Fuente, was not the authentic music of Walter's Grove. Reynolds always commented that Fuente came from the city of Terrance and wasn't native to the area where the Adrian and Kammara rivers met. Also, he was known as the King of Kammarice music and that style never left him even with his creation of Guanamamma music.

Piccanta music was the true music of Walter's Grove and Reynolds felt Guanamamma music had been an imposter. Thankfully, the Mango Nightclub was one of two nightclubs in the Roxie and Penelope District that played Guanamamma music on a regular basis. The Tajara was the other nightclub and without them, Latisha and I would not have had a place to perform Guanamamma dancing in the district.

"Are my favorite dancers ready to go?" Antonio Henderson said, after knocking on the door to enter our designated section.

"We are always ready," Latisha replied. "You know that."

Antonio smiled and brushed the pant legs of his peach jumpsuit. He wore the latest pastel-colored jumpsuits better than anyone I had seen in the city. Antonio was a tall, muscular-built man with night-colored skin and a perfectly groomed treetop-style haircut. He had an intimidating presence upon first glance but I had known him for years and he was really a gentle, soft-spoken man at heart.

The nightclub owner had allowed us to perform as the opener for the past four years. He had been a supporter of Guanamamma music and dancing, despite the rest of the nightclubs—besides The Tajara—playing Piccanta music exclusively. Antonio was a long-time friend of my father, Gustavoe, who danced at the Mango right up to his last days with us.

"I need your best performance tonight," Antonio said, while he straightened out the top part of his jumpsuit. "I'm swimming against what the people want these days. I had to stop my sound system man from playing Guanamamma music outside on the nights you're dancing. The crowd did not want to hear that old-time music, as they say, in this district anymore. I finally gave in and started having Piccanta music played outside to get the crowd we have for tonight."

"I cannot believe this monotonous, repetitive music has taken off the way that it has. Piccanta music is nothing but drums!" I shot back.

Antonio laughed. "Drums that move hips and behinds! People want to lose themselves in the music and dance the night away. You both are the last hope to show why Guanamamma music still matters. Your father did an admirable job standing up for our city's native music. Ciscoe, you have continued in that tradition. The times have changed since Diondray came to town and danced in our parking lot. His dance changed what the people wanted."

I sighed. Antonio was correct. Diondray Azur arrived in our city four years before and was on a quest to travel the entire land on both sides of the Great Forest. He had found a copy of the Book of Kammbi, a religious text, in his birth city of Charlesville. Charlesville was one of the four cities in this region, south of the Great Forest. The other cities were Adrian (northwest from here), and Terrance (southeast from here). Each city had its own character and were not really connected except for being in the same region. Diondray was going to change that due to the prophecy in the last chapter of the Book of Kammbi. The prophecy stated that a descendant of Oscar Ortega, the first disciple of the God Kammbi would unite both regions. Diondray had already traveled to the four cities north of the Great Forest (Santa Sophia, Santa Teresa, Alicia, & Issabella) and our city, Walter's Grove, was the second stop in the south region after Adrian. Diondray had connected immediately to Guanamamma music and dancing. Latisha and I met him for the first time at Darcie's, a level one nightclub a few streets east of the Mango. He wanted to learn how to dance to Guanamamma music and we taught him. His dance in the Mango parking lot before leaving our city was still talked about to this day. Many people believe that dance gave rise to Piccanta music and dancing and not Raphael Reynolds' proclamations. Diondray's dance was not what Latisha and I taught him. His dancing with our friend Donya Elena Herrera was closer to Piccanta dancing in many people's minds. It was something different for sure, especially when the leopards from the Great Forest came to watch them. But I contended that it was not Piccanta dancing either.

Latisha grabbed my right hand. "We will be ready, Antonio."

Antonio Henderson exited the designated section. I could not help but think that something might change after that night's performance.

"I do not want you to get lost in thought before we perform," Latisha said, and placed her hands on my face. "Dancing with your mind somewhere does not bring out the best in you. And as you heard, we are going to need our best for tonight. I need you to focus, my love."

I smiled at my wife. I believed she knew me better than I did myself at times. My mind had begun to drift towards thoughts about my father. He was adamant on the importance of keeping Guanamamma dancing around so that all the people of this city would always have a connection to its history. My father could have danced only in the West Walter's Grove district for the wealthy and made a better living. But he wanted to dance at the nightclubs in the Roxie and Penelope District here in the southeast section of the city to keep Guanamamma dancing connected to the working class people who came to enjoy themselves for a night out. I was committed to follow in his footsteps and that connection to him meant everything.

I placed my left hand on her dark brown right cheek and took a deep breath. She was still beautiful to me after sixteen years of marriage and now in our early forties. My light brown skin contrasted perfectly with her skin tone. She was a few inches taller than me but it never felt awkward that I always had to look up at her. I thought she would never marry a man as short as myself. Plus, our city viewed marriage quite loosely since our founder of the city, Walter Fuente, nearly 170 years ago had two wives. Monogamous relationships were not celebrated in Walter's Grove. Latisha demanded that if we got married, she would be the only one. I had not regretted the decision at all.

I ran my fingers through her close-cropped hairstyle and softly kissed her. She opened the door from the designated section and I watched the nightclub owner walk towards the stage. He glanced at us and gave that customary smile. It was time to show them what we got.

"Welcome to the best nightclub in the Roxie and Penelope District," Antonio announced over a microphone. He looked out at the patrons on the dance floor. "It's time to get your evening started with a performance from our resident dannzas, Ciscoe & Latisha Maldonado."

The patrons on the dance floor gave a polite clap. Latisha grabbed my hand again as we walked out from our designated section. I took a deep breath and started to visualize our dance. I looked over at the sound system man and he nodded.

The music came on and it was *You're Better Than a Glass of Javann* by Walter Fuente. This was our starter song each time we danced here at the Mango. The song had a whimsical and ironic tone about how a woman that Walter just met after a performance was better than the best glass of javann, our city's signature liquor. I always thought that song was a playful contrast to the rest of Fuente's music. It had a lively drum solo and the altophone horn gave the song a bouncy feel that I enjoyed dancing to.

I led Latisha through this first song of our set and she was in tune with me. Guanamamma dancing always began with the man leading in the back-and-forth step with his partner. My dad taught that this basic step was an invitation from a woman, if her male partner was good enough to lead. When I first started learning how to dance as a child, I never understood why Father viewed this basic step as such. However, I had come to understand after dancing with Latisha for all these years. I had to earn the invitation to lead Latisha in the dance and it always began with the basic back-and-forth step.

We did the back-and-forth step four times and returned to the base position. My guide hand, the right one, was in the middle of her back. I pressed my guide hand into her back gently and she knew it was her cue to slide to her right.

"You are here," Latisha said softly in my ear.

I nodded and returned to the back-and-forth step. The slide to the right was called the First Point of Guanamamma dancing. There were three points in Guanamamma dancing, like a triangle, and the goal was to reach all of them by the end of the song. Guanamamma music was created in a three-part song structure for dancing and once dancers understood that structure, the dance came naturally.

We reached the other two points by the end of the first song and heard a polite applause from the patrons. I had noticed the disinterest and indifferent looks on the patrons' faces while we danced the first song. Did they dislike Guanamamma dancing that much? Did it seem that out of touch with the partygoers in this district?

"Stay with me, my love," Latisha said, and squeezed my hand before we began the second song of our set.

"A disappointing response."

"Yes, my love. Keep going and don't drift away!"

I shook my head as *Blue Dress* by Diego Washington came on the sound system. *Blue Dress* was Washington's greatest hit song and told the story of how the narrator of the song met a mysterious woman wearing a blue dress in the Roxie and Penelope District. The narrator never knew her name or what part of the city she came from. However, she always showed up in the district wearing the same blue dress, wanting to dance Guanamamma. The song had a more relaxed sound than *You're Better Than a Glass of Javann* and I thought it was an excellent follow-up song for our set.

"Stay with me," Latisha said softly. "Don't look at the crowd."

I had to remain focused. Each time, I glanced at the crowd I noticed the blank stares and lukewarm smiles. I groaned inwardly and looked at Latisha. *Keep dancing, Ciscoe.*

"You are back. Let's finish the set!"

We finished dancing to the Washington song and heard the same polite applause as for the first song. I shook my head and got into position for our final song. We needed to dance our best. I glanced over at Antonio and saw him talking with Harrell and Brittany. They were dannzas that performed at several other nightclubs in the district. I had never seen them perform at the Mango. Did Antonio invite them to perform? We were always assured since we got this gig that Latisha and I would be the only opening performance at the Mango. Was this his reason for saying that we had to bring our best tonight?

One Night With You by Walter Fuente came on the sound system. I gathered myself and led Latisha in the back-and-forth step. *One Night With You* was Fuente's dedication song to his first wife, Josette, when they first met back in the city of Terrance. Josette passed away from an illness just before Walter Fuente came to the area and founded our city. She was the inspiration for a lot of his songs and this one had been considered the best of those types of songs. It was one of the oldest songs in his musical catalog and a great ending song for our set. The altophone horn and the timbau, a drum played between the musician's legs, carried the song.

"You are still my favorite short man with the best beard in Walter's Grove!"

I laughed and guided her to the right for the first point of the dance.

One night with you
Is all I wanted
Not just for a night of passion
Not just to take you to dinner
But just to be with you
To see your smile
To make you laugh
To have one night with you

Walter Fuente had a high, nasal voice and he always held the note at the end of each phrase during the song. I made sure to lead Latisha a step longer at each point of the dance. Guanamamma dancing had to be in sync with the music. This was not a dance to show off like Piccanta dancing. Dancing and music were meant to be in unison with each other. Piccanta music and dancing seemed like they always clashed every time I saw it. The dancing never connected with the music. It was more freestyle and loose. And I didn't understand why people coming to our district wanted that over Guanamamma music and dancing.

I saw your brown eyes and warm smile
And I had to meet with you
I had to find out
Who you were
Because you only get one chance
To meet someone
Like you

We made it to the second point of the dance. I led Latisha into several twirls as we moved forward like we were heading towards the point of the triangle. I kept looking at my wife and did not glance at the crowd or Antonio talking with Harrell and Brittany. I had to get through the set.

Walter Fuente had updated the song from the original Kammarice version back in Terrance. Fuente added the *pandretta*, a silver, hand-held percussion instrument that created a hand-clapping sound. The pandretta gave the updated version a festival-type of sound that I thought would energize the crowd. That did not happen. The energy from the patrons was the same as it was at the beginning of our set.

I returned to the back-and-forth step as I led Latisha into the third and final point of the dance. I raised my left hand to twirl her several times. I had to make sure to keep those twirls tight and use my right hand as the guide for the twirling. The right hand always remained in the middle of the back. It could never drift lower to her behind. Guanamamma dancing was not a sexual dance. Sex was for the bedroom, not the dance floor. Piccanta dancing made it all about sex. That kind of energy, which I enjoyed with my wife in its proper context, missed the point about dancing. Dancing was about communication and connection, not lust.

One night with you
Is all I wanted
I wanted to find out
About what you like
About what made you laugh
About the things you like to do
All I needed was one night
Could you grant me that wish
One night with you

An altophone horn solo finished the final verse as I twirled Latisha a couple more times and we returned to our base position. The song ended and I heard the same polite applause we had received at our introduction. I held Latisha and looked out at the patrons. Their lukewarm smiles said what they thought of our performance.

"Thank you, Ciscoe and Latisha, for your beautiful dancing to some Guanamamma classics," Antonio announced. "We have another performance for you coming up."

"Another performance?" I said to Antonio as we walked off the dance floor.

"Yes, another performance," he replied. "I said that I needed to see your best tonight. Competition is always waiting in the wings."

"That was not our agreement."

Antonio frowned. "Things have changed, my friends. And I have a club to run."

Latisha pulled me away from the dance floor or I would have stood there and argued with Antonio. I could not believe he would break his agreement with us all of a sudden. My father had worked out that Latisha and I would dance at his club two nights a week and there would not be any other dancing performances on our night of dancing. What had changed his mind now?

Harrell and Brittany walked passed us towards the dance floor. They did not belong here on our night. Harrell was a bald-headed, dark-skinned man with a gangly build. His companion, Brittany, was a petite, blond woman with a round frame.

"Surprised to see us!" Harrell remarked, his arm around Brittany's waist.

"Yes," I replied sharply.

"It's time to give people that come to the Mango what they want."

"What is that?"

Brittany laughed. "Not music and dancing of the past. No one wants that anymore."

"There is always a place for Guanamamma music and dancing," I retorted.

"Maybe you both can dance in the West Walter Grove District for those people," Harrell fired back. "Those rich folks will always like that old style of music and dancing."

Harrell and Brittany laughed and kept moving towards the dance floor. I could not believe what was happening. Latisha grabbed my hand again and led me back to the designated area.

"We just had our first performance of the evening. Now it's time for the final performance of the evening. Give Harrell and Brittany a big Mango Nightclub welcome as they dance to the current hit, *She's Got It* by Raphael Reynolds!" Antonio announced.

I heard the patrons applaud louder for Harrell and Brittany as we finished changing our clothes. Latisha and I came out from the designated area to watch them perform. The couple stood in position as the song came on the music player. Besides being the spokesperson for Piccanta music, Raphael Reynolds had created some of its most popular songs.

She's got it
She knows how to move
She's got it
She knows how to move
Dance for me, darling
Show everyone how to move your body
She's got it

The patrons clapped to the beat while Harrell and Brittany started with several back-and-forth steps. Piccanta dancing incorporated that Guanamamma step into the dance. He pulled Brittany closer and placed his hands on her wide hips. They both gyrated to the music.

Harrell smiled at the crowd and they applauded in return. Was this what they wanted?

She's got it
She knows how to move
Shake it for me, darling
Shake it for the music, darling
Shake it for our city
She's got it

Harrell dropped his hands from her hips and began to circle Brittany. She wore a skin-tight white dress that accentuated her hips and behind. Brittany gyrated seductively as Harrell continued to circle her. She reached out her left hand, Harrell grabbed it, and they returned to dancing close together. The patrons cheered and some of them began dancing just like Harrell and Brittany.

"That's not dancing. They are grinding against each other. There is no thought, no pattern, or elegance to Piccanta dancing. Just lazy!"

"I know, my love," Latisha said, and placed her arm around my waist. "There is still a place for Guanamamma dancing. This is just what the people want right now. We have to keep faith that the tide will turn back to the music and dancing that the city was founded on."

"Raphael Reynolds has challenged that assertion," I replied.

"He has, my love. But the truth will always come out in the end."

I looked over at Antonio and saw him smiling as the dance floor got crowded. He was into Harrell and Brittany's dancing and I could not deny that it got the crowd energized and ready for another night of partying at the Mango.

"That was Harrell and Brittany Delaware performing to *She's Got It* by Raphael Reynolds. Thank you, Harrell and Brittany, for your performance."

The crowd clapped loudly as the couple took a bow.

"That's the kind of energy I need to get my patrons going," Antonio said to us as he came back to the designated section.

"I thought you agreed to not having another dannza couple perform on the nights we danced?" I replied.

Antonio frowned. "I'm sorry, Ciscoe. I did agree to those terms as a favor to your father. He wanted you to continue what he started many years ago. However, I had no choice in having Harrell and Brittany perform tonight."

"What do you mean you had no choice?" Latisha interjected. "This is your nightclub."

"All I can tell you is that I was forced to have Harrell and Brittany perform tonight. The nightclub is all that I have and I cannot lose it."

"Cannot lose it?" I said. "How could you lose the nightclub?"

"Maybe you both should consider dancing to Piccanta music. This is the music of the district now. Guanamamma music does not have a place here anymore. Ciscoe, I know you would rather dance here than up in the West Walter's Grove District. You may have to consider dancing in that district, if you want to keep dancing Guanamamma."

"I want to dance here in this district. Not for those people. You know that!"

"I know. However, I'm replacing your performance for Harrell and Brittany's performance effective tonight. I have a business to run and my patrons are my main priority. I have the best Level One Nightclub in the district. And we cannot live in the past anymore. Thank you for dancing for the past four years. But it's time for a change."

"Time for a change!" I fired back. "You promised that Guanamamma music and dancing would always have a place here."

Antonio sighed. "I'm not a man to break agreements, especially to those I consider friends. But times have changed. Mango Nightclub has to change with them. I have to keep up with the other Level One Nightclubs like The Tajara and Darcie's for patrons. I'm truly sorry. Both of you are always welcome here at the Mango."

I did not understand what outside person would make Antonio go back on his word and fire us from the Mango. What in the world was going on? I grabbed our stuff from the designated section and we left the nightclub.

Chapter 2

I only slept for a few hours after what happened with Antonio at the Mango Nightclub that night. Latisha attempted to keep my spirits high with her usual brand of encouragement. But I did not take to her encouraging words and she went to sleep not long after we got home. I called Antonio after waking up and tried to find out who had forced him to have Harrell and Brittany perform at the Mango. Antonio answered the phone and said he could not tell me who had forced him to make that decision. The Mango meant everything to him and he could not lose it. But I wondered, who would force him to do that? The other Level One Nightclub owners? Raphael Reynolds? It did not make any sense and we were out of a job.

I cooked breakfast and got ready to practice our routine for the Festival of Josette. We were also teaching Guanamamma dancing at the Fuente Center later in the day. Fuente Center was the biggest park in our district, East Walter's Grove. Latisha and I started teaching there when Diondray was in the city four years before. It was the first time we had an open practice for the people of our district to show why Guanamamma dancing still mattered. We had been teaching at Fuente Center once a week since our first session and I was glad to see people wanting to learn how to dance to the city's native music.

It was the twenty-fifth day in the six month of Une and we were thirty days away from the city's biggest festival. Latisha and I were going to perform at the Festival of Josette for the third year in a row. We were able to perform on the last day of the festival for the Guanamamma Extravaganza at the Josette Arena in the Roxie and Penelope District. Our performance showcased the history of Guanamamma music and dancing for the city. My father started that performance ten years before when he was still alive. He noticed back then that people of the city started losing the connection to the history of Guanamamma music and dancing. He did not want the people of the city to lose that connection to our history. I had promised him in his last days with us that I would always keep that connection to our music alive for everyone. Performing in the Guanamamma Extravaganza had become the highlight for me each year.

I was stretching before practice and the phone rang.

"Antonio called me last night after talking to you and kept apologizing for what he had to do," Delia Villanueva said firmly.

Delia was the city's richest woman because of the ownership and sale of Manrique Liquors. She helped build the city's largest liquor company, alongside her late husband, Manrique Villanueva. She sold the company to Azur Liquors a year after his death and had then become the city's biggest socialite. I had known her since childhood. Delia was a close friend of my father and used her influence to get him to perform at The Festival of Josette. I had become the beneficiary of that same influence as well.

"Why would he break the agreement?" I asked. "I remember when he shook my hand after talking to Gustavoe about Latisha and I dancing at the Mango."

"Gustavoe told me about it the next day. He was not well and knew he did not have many more days left with us. I heard how proud he was of you over the phone. I reminded Antonio of that conversation and what it means to perform at the Mango. You don't go back on your word like that."

"Who would make him go back on his word?"

"Darcie is behind this." Delia said sharply.

"How could she make Antonio decide to allow another dannza couple to perform on the same night as us? And why would our performance cause us to get fired? She doesn't have that kind of power in the Roxie and Penelope District."

"You should know how persuasive she can be. I heard that she is dating Raphael Reynolds."

"She is," I interjected. "I did not think she would date one man exclusively. But they both hate Guanamamma music and dancing, so it should not surprise me they're together."

"Correct, Ciscoe. Also, you know she blames you for allowing Diondray Azur to leave Walter's Grove. She was in love with him."

I shook my head. "How could she be in love with someone almost half her age? We're almost the same age and Diondray is a man in his twenties. She knew he was not going to stay in Walter's Grove because of that prophecy from the Book of Kammbi."

"You should know that age doesn't matter when it comes to love in this city," Delia retorted. "I'm sixty-three and the women in my social group are all dating several men at a time who are half their age. That's nothing new and Darcie loves fast and hard. She did with you all those years ago. I'm glad that relationship ended. I never felt she was right for you. And you know how much she hates the Book of Kammbi and what those beliefs represent. She is determined to get revenge on you for allowing him to leave Walter's Grove."

"She does love fast and hard. Hates the same way too. I hope she will not try to get us removed from performing at the Festival of Josette."

"Darcie may have a relationship with Raphael Reynolds and try to influence him to remove you and Latisha from dancing at The Festival of Josette. But I will not let that happen."

"Thank you, Delia. Your support has meant a lot to me over the years."

"Always, Ciscoe. I made a promise to your father and I will never break it. Supporting you for all of these years has been the best decision of my life."

I held the phone in my right hand after Delia hung up. Supporting me had been the best decision of her life. What did she mean by that? And what did I need to find out? I put aside her comments and got ready for practice.

Latisha and I did not have a good practice. My mind was distracted by what happened the night before with Antonio and the last part of my conversation with Delia on the phone earlier. We ended the practice quicker than usual before we got angrier at each other.

I was trying to understand why supporting me was the best decision of her life. If that was the case, then why not tell me? Was there some secret I needed to know about our relationship?

"Whatever it is she wants you to know, it will come out at the right time," Latisha said as we dressed for the teaching session at the Fuente Center.

"It seems odd that she would make a comment like that after we got fired from the Mango. Why now?"

"Things from the past always come unexpectedly," my wife replied. "I do agree with you about the timing. Maybe she is finally ready for you to know."

Latisha and I arrived at Fuente Center a few minutes later. Donya Elena had a dance floor built on the east side of the main building. It rained hard for our first teaching session four years ago. But we got a covering built over the dance floor a year later and then we could practice anytime, despite the weather.

"Dancing Guanamamma is all about communication and connection to you and your partner," I stated, as we began the teaching session. There were nine couples in attendance. Latisha walked by each couple to make sure they had the correct posture. "That's why I always begin each teaching session without music first. Learning the dance without music creates that initial connection to yourself and your partner."

"Mr. Maldonado, I learned in my Piccanta dancing lesson a couple of days ago that you should always dance to the music. The music will create that connection with your partner. Your body needs to be attuned to the music at all times," Frank Parris said.

Frank Parris and his partner, Valencia, were on the first row to the right of me. He was a tall, pencil-thin man with long-flowing brown hair and an artist's sensibility about him. Valencia was nearly as tall, but all curves to offset his angles. They looked like an odd couple for Guanamamma dancing, but I have learned over the years that dancing can bring the unlikeliest people together.

"Piccanta dancing gets it wrong," I countered, as I felt my wife's eyes from the other side of the dance floor. "They want dancers to get lost in the music. Guanamamma dancing is not about getting lost in the music. The music is there to support the dance between you and your partner. Because if you lose yourself in the music, then you will lose that connection to your dance partner."

I glanced at Latisha after my reply and saw a small smile on her face. I had just warded off a discussion in the car after the teaching session.

Just as we were getting started to dance without music, I saw another couple coming onto the dance floor.

"My deepest apologies for being late, Mr. Maldonado," a short, plump man said, with his partner standing next to him. The partner was the same height and body type as the man who just spoke. "This is our first time in this district and we got lost a bit before we found the Fuente Center."

"I told him how to get here from the directions Ms. Herrera gave us. But of course, he did not want to listen," the partner added.

Laughter erupted from the other couples as that scenario was quite common between partners in following directions to find a place.

"I did not know we were going to have another couple with us for the teaching session," I replied. "Being on time is important in Guanamamma dancing. Because tardiness is contagious."

"We are sorry, Mr. Maldonado. I will make sure Parvah and I are on time going forward," the woman said.

"Make sure you are…"

"Bismilla Gancha is my name and he is Parvah Bandha. We are from the Viddhana people that live in the South Walter's Grove District. We found out from Ms. Herrera that you and your wife taught Guanamamma dancing. Parvah and I want to learn this type of dancing because it is close to our own traditional Viddhana dancing."

"We will talk after the teaching session," I interrupted. "Get in position and follow along."

"They don't belong here," Frank Parris interjected. "Those people live amongst themselves and never participate in anything with the other districts of the city. They don't allow anyone else from the city to come to their portion of the district they live in."

I glanced at the other couples and sensed they agreed with his comment. "First of all, Latisha and I will decide who can learn from our teaching sessions. Guanamamma dancing is for everyone in the city. We will not tolerate any student making other students unwelcome in our class. If anyone has a problem with that, you can leave. We will not teach anyone who has those kinds of feelings within their hearts."

I looked across the dance floor to see if anyone would leave. The other couples stood in their places. However, Frank Parris grabbed Valencia's arm to leave. She was not moving.

"You can go, Frank," Latisha added. "I will make sure Valencia has a ride home."

Frank Parris walked off angrily. Latisha took his place as Valencia's partner. I saw Bismilla and Parvah smile at me.

"It's time to dance," I said. "Pay attention, everyone!"

I instructed the couples through the entire three points of Guanamamma dancing without music. I wanted to make sure the men had their guide hands in the correct place and the women felt comfortable being led by their partners. We went through the entire dance several times before I played the music. The dance was not just about the music, as my father would say all the time. The dance became the connection between you and your partner.

"Thank you for making us feel welcome," Bismilla said, after the teaching session ended. It lasted a little over an hour. I could tell the rest of the couples were exhausted after my teaching. "Guanamamma dancing is so much like our traditional dance. Parvah and I were in tune to those steps quickly."

Parvah nodded as she spoke. "Yes, Mr. Maldonado. Guanamamma dancing felt liked we have danced like this all of our lives."

"Both of you look no older than twenty-five. How long have you been dancing your traditional dance?"

"You are correct, Mr. Maldonado," Parvah answered. "I'm twenty-three and Bismilla is twenty-four. We have been dancing traditional Viddhana since we were five years old. Our people believe that is the age when we can start learning how to dance."

"What made you both decide to come to this teaching session? It has been known the Viddhana people stay amongst themselves in the city."

Bismilla frowned. "This is correct, Mr. Maldonado. But people of our age want to be a part of the city. The Viddhana people have been here for several generations now and it's time to connect with the rest of the city. We cannot just stay amongst ourselves in order to keep our heritage alive."

Parvah nodded again. "Many of our people believe if we leave our neighborhood, we will lose our heritage and become assimilated into the city. Our parents and grandparents don't want what happened to the Nerdann tribe to happen to the Viddhana people. How can we lose our heritage when it is so much a part of who we are? Our people have something to add to this city and we are ready to be part of it."

Bismilla and Parvah made interesting points. The young Viddhana people did not want to do things the same way as those who came before them. But I did understand their parents' and grandparents' concern. Maintaining tradition and heritage was the responsibility of the elders of that culture. It was easy to lose it when the youth want to be part of what's happening in the present. The Nerdann tribe was a good example of how a people can lose their culture to assimilation. This city would not have been created without Walter Fuente's connection to that tribe.

If there were other young Viddhana people like Bismilla and Parvah that wanted to venture out to the rest of the city, then holding onto their traditions and heritage would become more challenging for sure.

***

"Look at this next-to-last sentence on this statue. *This will be a city built from a spirit of music, dance, and love.* I agree with Mr. Fuente's sentiment, but when you steal music from the native people of this city is that really love?" Raphael Reynolds said, in front of a crowd at the Wall of Walter's Declaration.

"Walter Fuente is a thief!" someone from the crowd yelled.

Raphael was a short, dark-skinned man with long braided hair and a commanding presence. The other people in the crowd agreed with that false statement and started to repeat it. I could not believe what I was hearing. How could they believe that the founder of our city was someone who stole music? Did they not understand how he included the Nerdann tribe's music into his musical style? Did they not understand how he honored their music and dance by paying homage to it in songs like *My Inspiration* and *This Music Gave Me Life*?

"Raphael Reynolds is spreading propaganda once again to everyone here," I blurted out, as I walked up to the front of the crowd at the Wall of Walter's Declaration. The crowd stopped shouting that false statement and turned towards me.

"I see that one of Walter Fuente's true diehards has joined us. Well, Ciscoe, can you explain how the truth I share with the people is propaganda from your perspective?" Raphael countered, as he held the timbau drum.

Wall of Walter's Declaration was a large slab of stone that stood several feet high and had a life-sized painting of Walter Fuente smiling with his arms around two women, Roxie Pierponte and Penelope Mentz. It was Walter and his two wives. They represented his new life here in this part of the region, South of the Great Forest. The landmark stood at the intersection of Ave Roxie and Ave Penelope in the Roxie and Penelope District. It was one of the main attractions of the district outside of the nightclubs and always had a crowd around it. I had dropped off Latisha to work at her brother Saahib's restaurant for the day and saw the crowd gathered around the landmark. I had to stop and find out why the crowd was there.

"Walter Fuente was inspired by Nerdann tribe's music. He wanted a new sound for the Kammarice music that came from Terrance. The tribe members accepted him when he arrived into this region and allowed the timbau drum as well as the pandretta to create Guanamamma music. Do you know that, Raphael?"

The crowd grumbled after my response.

Raphael laughed and responded. "Do you hear that ladies and gentlemen? I never thought the great dancer, Ciscoe Maldonado, who was born and raised in the East Walter's Grove District would buy into the lie that Walter Fuente's inspiration of Nerdann tribe's sound gave him license to create this stolen music called Guanamamma. Sounds like you went to school in the West Walter's Grove District and learn that falsehood very well. I have two members of the tribe to refute your claim."

There were two Nerdann tribe members with Raphael. They stood on each side of the musician with their timbau drums between their legs. Raphael always had tribe members play music with him. He wanted to show the people of the city that Piccanta music had not discarded the tribe members like Walter Fuente supposedly did during his time. Both tribe members had disapproving looks on their faces and one to the left of Raphael said, "Walter Fuente did not create a new music when he arrived here. He took our music and made it his own. The Nerdann tribe must set the record straight. "

The crowd returned to yelling that Walter Fuente was a thief.

I shook my head. "It's sad that Raphael is misleading everyone including members of the Nerdann tribe. Guanamamma music and dancing gave this city its own music and it has lasted a long time. Inauthentic music like Piccanta can never replace it!"

Raphael frowned and waved his hands to quiet the crowd. "Inauthentic music like Piccanta? I will show you what's inauthentic music to this city." He placed the timbau drum between his legs and began slapping it rapidly. The tribe members followed him. It created a fast, scattershot sound and I saw some in the crowd begin moving to it.

People of this city have always moved to the sound of the timbau
The Timbau tells the real story of our city
Not a second-rate music by someone that came from the east
The Timbau gets everybody to move
The Timbau gets everybody to groove
Because the tribe created that sound
And gave birth to the real music of this city
And it didn't need a guitar, piano, or altophone horn
Not like that music from the east
That made people dance
Like a rod was stuck in their backs
Now everybody say Piccanta!

The crowd said *Piccanta* after Raphael had sung that verse. The tribe members played timbau drum hard and fast. People were dancing Piccanta style and Raphael had everyone in the palm of his hand. There was no way I was going to convince anyone of correct history or how Walter Fuente created Guanamamma music amongst these people.

Now everybody say Piccanta!
Piccanta!
Piccanta!

Raphael Reynolds was a terrific timbau drum player and the backing of the tribe members enhanced their sound. Most of the crowd was dancing and getting lost in the music. I did not see any precision or coordinated steps. Just bodies joined together and dancing like dogs in heat. I had seen enough. If the people who came to this district to enjoy a night on the town could be swayed this easily, then Guanamamma music and dancing had an uphill climb in order to recapture the minds and behinds of this city.

Chapter 3

We danced at The Tajara Nightclub every fifth day of the week. The fifth day of the week was usually the nightclub's slowest night. The Tajara Nightclub was the last Level One Nightclub on the main street of Ave Roxie in the Roxie and Penelope District. The Level One Nightclubs were considered the best nightclubs in the district and attracted the most patrons who wanted to enjoy a night on the town. I had to drive pass Darcie's and the Mango Nightclub as we entered the district from the north. Percy Braxton, owner of The Tajara, did not want his nightclub next to the other two Level One Nightclubs and believed he had an advantage over them because of where it resided. The Tajara became the nightclub many patrons ended up for the rest of the evening after visiting Mango or Darcie's or some of the Level Two Nightclubs.

Percy Braxton wanted Guanamamma music and dancing played at his nightclub. He had opened The Tajara a couple of years before and heard about our dancing at the Mango. Percy was a friend of Delia and they had created a similar agreement to ours with Antonio at his nightclub. After what had happened over the past two days, I felt uneasy about performing at The Tajara that night. My thoughts went from getting fired at the Mango to Frank Parris leaving our teaching session to Raphael Reynolds' impromptu performance at the Wall of Walter's Declaration. I was not in the right frame of mind for our performance. It felt like the people of my beloved city had decided to push out Guanamamma music and dancing. My father always told me that Walter Fuente wanted this music and dancing to be the thing that brought everyone together. I didn't think that sentiment was true anymore and if we got rejected at The Tajara after our performance, then we would only have The Festival of Josette left to showcase our tradition.

The patrons of The Tajara were more receptive to Guanamamma dancing than they were at the Mango. The Tajara had an L-shaped layout and the dance floor was at the end of the L near the back. You had to walk down a long hallway and turn left before you got to the dance floor. We were allowed to set up in the back room near the dance floor before that night's performance. Latisha smiled and placed her hands on my face. I gave her a kiss and knew it was time to focus on our performance for the night. We still had a place to perform Guanamamma dancing and must show these patrons that it still mattered.

***

"Welcome to The Tajara, the finest nightclub in the Roxie and Penelope!" Percy Braxton announced over the microphone. He was a tall, sharply-dressed man with a regal presence. He always wore a pristine white jumpsuit and shiny black shoes. Percy stood almost seven feet tall and carried himself like he was the regnator of the city. We had just elected a new regnator, Hassan Felipe Montoya, last year. Many people thought Percy Braxton should have run against him to become the leader of our city. However, the wealthy that lived in the West Walter's Grove District would never allow a nightclub owner to become regnator of our city. Especially one with jet-black skin like Percy Braxton, no matter how well he dressed or presented himself to the public.

"I'm delighted to welcome our regular dannzas, Ciscoe and Latisha Maldonado, to get our evening started at The Tajara. Please give them a warm welcome as they dance to the Walter Fuente classic, *Kammara, Kammara.*"

The patrons had filled a section in front of the dance floor. They gave us a solid applause much better than we received at the Mango. Percy walked off the dance floor as we entered from the left.

Kammara, Kammara
Your water is so blue
Your water is so vast
I long to cross you
Like Hendric did all those years ago.
Kammara, Kammara
Your waves are calling me
Entering my dreams
Like a distant lover that I want to be with
Kammara, Kammara
I long to cross you

I chose *Kammara, Kammara* as our song for that night's performance at The Tajara. I did not want to do our normal three-song set. Latisha and I discussed in practice that we wanted to do one song for the patrons of The Tajara. I felt we needed to dance to our best song for our performance. *Kammara, Kammara* was the song we had danced the most for all the years we had been together.

Kammara, Kammara was considered one of Walter Fuente's most popular songs. This was the last major song he updated from the original Kammarice version into a Guanamamma version. He sang about the Kammara Sea and how the first voyager, Hendric Terrance Goltz crossed it for the first time and landed in the area that would become the city of Terrance. Even though the Kammara Sea was several hours east of our city, I connected with this song and Fuente's love for that body of water. The song began with a wailing altophone horn sound that seemed like a call out to sea. I led Latisha in the back-and-forth step after the altophone horn ended. We did our customary steps four times before heading into the first point of the dance as Walter began to sing.

Kammara, Kammara
Your water is so blue
Your water is so vast
Will I ever cross you?
Kammara, Kammara
I come to the beach
And stare as far as my eyes can see
I hope that Megaro, the Sea God
Is not there
Kammara, Kammara
The Sea God controls everyone
That tries to cross this vast blue sea
Maybe I will be the first one
To cross into the beyond
Without the Sea God controlling me

This song spoke about Megaro, the Sea God who controlled the Kammara Sea. It was said the gods who ruled that part of the region, South of the Great Forest, for generations, created the city of Terrance. We knew about the goddess Marrimba here in Walter's Grove because of her connection to Walter Fuente. She gave him the vision to start a new city. The story went that Megaro, the Sea God, was her younger brother and ruled the Kammara Sea. He was looking for a voyager from the east that would believe in the Sea God as the only true god of that region. Hendric Goltz was the first voyager that agreed to the Sea God's wishes in order to cross the Kammara Sea. However, the voyager wanted to return to the east after landing in the area that would become the city of Terrance. Goltz became homesick and pleaded with Megaro that he might return to his homeland. The Sea God refused Goltz's requests many times and the voyager decided to return without Megaro's blessing. Hendric was killed out at sea by Megaro because of his action. Walter's song paid homage to the Sea God's power and Goltz's determination to return home.

We made it to the second point after I twirled Latisha four times in step with the music. She smiled at me and knew I was focused. I glanced away to notice the patrons staring at us as we danced. I saw a couple mimicking our back-and-forth steps and twirling their partner. Several other couples were mouthing Walter's words. I got a much better vibe from the audience than the one at the Mango. I started to feel better about the performance.

"It is going to be alright, my love," Latisha whispered in my ear as we moved to the third point in the dance.

Kammara, Kammara
Your water is so vast
Your water is so blue
I want to stare at you forever
Will Megaro let me cross you
Like The First Voyager
However, I don't want to worship
The Sea God
I want to cross the sea
And go as far as the ship will take me

Kammara, Kammara
Kammara, Kammara
Please take me away

"That was Ciscoe and Latisha Maldonado getting our evening started here at The Tajara. Thank you for dancing to one of the greatest Guanamamma songs that has been ever recorded, *Kammara, Kammara,*" the announcer said, standing near the sound system in the corner of the dance floor.

The patrons clapped much louder than they did at the Mango. Latisha and I bowed before leaving the dance floor. Guanamamma dancing still had a place in the Roxie and Penelope District.

We walked back to Percy's office and saw him talking on the phone as we tried to enter the room. He held up his hand indicating that we had to wait before we could enter the office. He was having an intense discussion. Percy closed the door to continue the discussion.

"Let's go eat," Latisha said.

I got an odd feeling that we had something to do with the conversation he was having on the phone.

"We danced great tonight, no matter what happens," I said softly.

My wife nodded as we left the nightclub. However, I wanted to know who Percy was talking to on the phone and hoped the same thing would not happen as it did at the Mango.

We crossed the street from The Tajara and walked a block east to Ave Evelyn to our favorite restaurant, *Saahib's.* Many patrons came to eat at the restaurant after a night of partying. It was the main eating establishment of the Roxie and Penelope District.

"Hello Sis and brother-in-law. You both are a little early tonight," Saahib said, as he seated us at the back of the restaurant.

My brother-in-law, Saahib Harrell, had the same dark brown

complexion as his sister. He was a couple of inches taller than Latisha and looked like her twin even though he was four years younger.

"We just finished dancing at The Tajara and I thought it was time to leave early," Latisha answered.

Saahib frowned. "I heard what happened at the Mango. I thought Antonio would let you both dance Guanamamma for as long as you wanted."

"I thought the same, brother-in-law," I interjected. "He made a promise to both us and my father that Guanamamma music and dancing would always have a place at the Mango."

A waitress brought our food and drinks to the table. We never had to order food from the restaurant. Saahib knew I wanted tortas every time we came to eat. Tortas were mango slices, corn, and finger-shaped beef strips laid on a piece of circular, chalky, white bread. The bread absorbed the juices from the mango, corn, and beef to make it extra chewy. Delicious. My father made the best tortas and would always comment that it was the best thing that came from the city of Adrian. Adrian was known for the liquor called Javann but my father did not drink. Tortas was our main food at home and I had never got tired of eating them all these years later. Saahib made them just as well as my father did and he always provided a full plate each time we came here after dancing. Latisha always wanted the Bohanni dish that consisted of steamed collard greens covered by yellow rice, blackberries, and grilled chicken. Also, Saahib created a spicy Bohanni sauce that added an extra kick to the dish. The Bohanni dish had become a favorite of the nightclub patrons and Saahib always made sure to have a fresh plate for his big sister every time we came to eat. I liked the Bohanni dish, but not over Tortas.

"Our city is losing our connection," Saahib lamented, after the waitress left the table. "I will admit that I like Piccanta music but we cannot push away Guanamamma music."

"Do you like *She's Got It* over *Kammara, Kammara?*" I shot back after taking my first bite of the tortas.

"My love," Latisha interjected.

Saahib raised his hand to stop my wife. "It's okay, Sis. I know how passionate brother-in-law gets about this subject. Of course, I believe *Kammara, Kammara* is a much better song than *She's Got It.* However, that song gets people dancing and has great energy."

"Saahib is correct, my love. The people love that song and others like it. You know people want to let loose these days. No one wants to dance Guanamamma anymore."

"People want to get lost in the drums and percussion these days, brother-in-law. They don't want to think or listen intently to the music. Piccanta music lets people get loose."

"Thanks for the encouragement, Saahib. At least your tortas are still great."

Saahib placed his left hand on my right shoulder. "I know what this music means to you. You can always dance at those parties in the West Walter's Grove District. Those rich folks still love Guanamamma."

I sighed and finished my food. "I know, brother-in law. Those house parties don't have the same energy as here in the Roxie and Penelope. I don't fit in with those people in the West Walter's Grove District. My people are here but they don't like Guanamamma anymore."

Saahib nodded. "You are still dancing at The Festival of Josette. I hope you can keep dancing there every year."

"There you are."

"You were looking for us, Ralph," I replied.

Ralph Johnson was one of the security people employed at The Tajara. He looked every bit the part for his job. He had a muscular build that filled out his blue uniform. Ralph's bald head and piercing eyes created an intimidating presence that kept everything in order at The Tajara.

"Percy wanted you to have this," Ralph continued, and handed me an envelope. "See you around."

Ralph had a blank look on his face as he turned to leave the restaurant. I opened the envelope and read the letter.

"What it is, my love?"

"We just got removed from The Festival of Josette."

Chapter 4

The Festival of Josette was the city's biggest festival and lasted for six days, beginning on the twenty-fifth day in the seventh month of Yul. It celebrated the founding of the city by Walter Leonardo Fuente, nearly 170 years ago.

The Festival of Josette celebrated Walter's journey from Terrance to Walter's Grove and the beliefs that honored his change in musical style, the importance of dancing, and the right of a person to love anyone they wanted. The festival always opened with the reading of the Wall of Walter's Declaration and played his most controversial song, *What You See In the Light Is Not What You Think.* That song revealed his marriage to two wives, Roxanne Pierponte and Penelope Mentz, and exposed the Konzill members (Terrance's City Council) that were planning to marry multiple wives. The musician affirmed his marriage in that song, despite the Monogamy Act passed into law by the Regnator of Terrance, Syonne.

Syonne wanted Walter Fuente to annul his marriage to one of those women in order to keep his status as the greatest musician in the city of Terrance. Fuente refused and was forced to leave his birth city for good. The Festival of Josette used Walter's Declaration and that song as a springboard to celebrate Walter's Grove as a city different than rigid, uptight Terrance. I had always looked forward to the festival and getting to perform in it for the last two years had been one of the highlights of my life. Now, it was being taken away.

Latisha and I had arrived at Delia's house the next morning after our practice, trying to get some answers on why we were removed from The Festival of Josette.

Delia lived in West Walter's Grove District, which had the most luxurious homes in the city. Most of the homes were made in the Bremen style where the top formed into a triangle and had decorative columns, while the bottom half of the home was nondescript. The top half of the Bremen style homes in the district was where each homeowner showed their creativity and ostentatiousness. Each year there was a contest in the district to see which Bremen style home had the most creative top half of their house. The winner would be talked about in the district for that year.

Delia's home was in a plain Bremen style and her top half looked exactly like the bottom half. She always told me that the interior of her home mattered more than the exterior. Delia had become well known to the people of the district because of her late husband, Manrique Villanueva. Together, they threw lavish parties for the people of the district and their signature liquor, *Manrique,* was the drink of choice. That liquor connected them to the wealthy and government officials of the city and turned Delia into a socialite.

"Good to see you both again." Delia said, after we were brought into the living room by her butler, Hernando.

Delia Villanueva was an elegant, petite woman who always dressed impeccably every time I saw her. If Percy Braxton was the best-dressed man I had ever seen, then Delia matched him as the best-dressed woman. She had shoulder-length black hair with grey streaks. Most women of that district would have gotten rid of the grey streaks in their hair. Not Delia. She was proud of her grey hair and it did not take away from her elegance.

"Why are we getting removed from The Festival of Josette?" I said, as we sat on a large red velvet couch. I handed her the letter I got from Ralph Johnson.

Delia read the letter quickly and closed it. "The letter is stating that all three Level One Nightclub owners have agreed with Raphael Reynolds that Guanamamma music and dancing should not be played at their nightclubs anymore because this music was stolen from Nerdann tribe, the original people of this city. The Level One Nightclub owners support Raphael Reynolds' petition to the Civita for the removal of all aspects of Walter Fuente's creation of Guanamamma music and those who are closely aligned with it from The Festival of Josette. If we are going to celebrate the city's musical and dancing heritage, then Piccanta music and dancing should be the only music featured at the festival."

"Unbelievable! He's gone to the Civita to carry out this falsehood."

"Raphael believes deeply about Piccanta music, as you do about Guanamamma music," Latisha said.

Delia nodded at her comment.

"That letter is lying. Walter Fuente founded this city and Guanamamma music upon his arrival from Terrance. He did not steal this music from the Nerdann tribe. Raphael Reynolds has gone too far with his propaganda against our music. How can you have the biggest festival in this city and remove the music Walter Fuente created?" I replied.

"Raphael Reynolds is determined to get Guanamamma music and dancing removed from this city," Delia said. "He has lost all perspective on this city's history."

"He knows that Walter Fuente came from the city of Terrance and connected first with the Nerdann tribe upon his arrival. He had tribe members in his band. Those tribe elders would not let him have those members in the band, if he had stolen their music," Latisha added. "Raphael Reynolds has to know that history. It is chronicled at the Civita. The Civita members can show him the letters Walter Fuente wrote when he first arrived. How can people believe Guanamamma music was stolen?"

"Exactly, my love. The Civita has all of those letters and anyone in the city can request to see them. Is Raphael Reynolds refuting those letters?"

"What proof would he have to refute those letters?" Delia countered. "I will talk to my contact in the Civita to make sure you both are allowed to perform at The Festival of Josette. Don't worry, Ciscoe. I know what this means to you. You are just like Gustavoe when it comes to Guanamamma."

"I'm just like my father?"

Delia smiled. "Of course, Ciscoe. You take after him when it comes to Guanamamma. You believe exactly like him when it comes to the dancing."

My wife chuckled and stated, "Communication and connection are the essence of dancing Guanamamma. How you move your feet and lead your partner is what the dance is about."

"Well, that's true," I replied.

"We know, Ciscoe," Delia interjected. "Gustavoe was the same way. He taught you well."

Latisha nodded at that comment. "He sure did, my love."

My father emphasized that communication and connection were essential to Guanamamma dancing. I would get corrected immediately if he saw that I was leading my partner incorrectly during a dance. My posture had to be correct. My hands had to be in the correct position. I always learned to reach the three points of the dance without music with every teaching session taught by him. My father did not want me to get lost in the music or swayed by the lyrics. Guanamamma dancing needed to represent the music as its equal not just something created to have sex with as many women as possible. I had to admit that strident belief from my father was at odds with the city's culture. I wanted to learn how to Guanamamma dance as a young adult to get with as many women as I could. The Wall of Walter's Declaration did state that his city would be founded with a spirit of love. However, I began to see my father's beliefs as my own as I got older. And being married and monogamous to Latisha for so many years had augmented my own beliefs about this dancing.

"My father was correct and Guanamamma dancing is about communication and connection," I said. "Did you see how Harrell and Brittany danced with each other at the Mango? That is not dancing. They might as well have sex on the dance floor!"

Delia blushed. "I did not want to get you started. The tone of your voice even sounds like Gustavoe. The apple does not fall far from the tree."

Both women laughed. I did sound like my father. He was the most important person in my life before I met Latisha. His love for Guanamamma music and dancing was genuine and I planned to do everything I could to keep it alive in the city.

I caressed my wife's hand and sighed. "We had a young Viddhana couple come to our teaching session yesterday. I was surprised they would come to our district. The young woman of the couple shared that traditional Viddhana dance was similar to Guanamamma dancing. And by the way they were dancing, I believed her. If the Viddhana people have a dance similar to Guanamamma dancing, then it can show how it was meant for everyone in Walter's Grove. And if Walter Fuente had stolen this music from the Nerdann tribe, then it would not have connected to another group of people in the city."

Delia gave a small smile. "I know the young Viddhana people want to be a part of this city. They refuse to believe they would lose their culture if they interacted more with everyone else."

"If we can show the Civita that the Viddhana people have embraced Guanamamma music and dancing, then we can make the claim it truly does represent the city. Stolen music cannot do that." I stated.

"Correct, Ciscoe," Delia added. "You both will dance at The Festival of Josette. I promised your father that I would uphold that position for you. And he has my word on that."

***

If a man wants to marry more than one wife, it will be allowed in this city. I will never create or allow anyone else to create a law prohibiting anyone from loving as many people as he or she wants. This will be a city built from a spirit of music, dance, and love. Nothing else. I declare it on this day, the eighth of Nayur, the first month in the Year 94 A.O.A.

"Those were the first words I read when I arrived in Walter's Grove," Morrim Airto Goinz said in the sanctuary at Kahall Azur. Kahall Azur was built two years prior in the East Walter's Grove District. Latisha and I had been attending Book of Kammbi teachings at least once a week since Morrim Goinz and several diakonos came to Walter's Grove three years before. They came ninety days after Diondray Azur left Walter's Grove. Diakono Malcolm Copperwith returned to Walter's Grove after Diondray left Terrance for his birth city, Charlesville. He laid the groundwork for Morrim Goinz and the other diakonos to come to Walter's Grove. Latisha and I had been the only parishioners for the past two years. We allowed Morrim Goinz to share the teachings from The Book of Kammbi from our home until Kahall Azur was built.

It was the first time any of them had ever been to any city south of the Great Forest. Their presence in the city had not been a smooth transition. Most citizens fundamentally rejected their teachings and wanted them to leave Walter's Grove. The Book of Kammbi and its teachings stood in opposition to the Wall of Walter's Declaration. However, Kahall Azur had gained more people to hear Morrim Goinz teach from that sacred book. More people from that district than any of the others in the city were becoming believers and followers of Kammbi. I always knew there would be a longing by people in this city for something more than Walter's Declaration. If Latisha and I connected with the teachings from The Book of Kammbi, then others could as well. I didn't agree with everything written in The Book of Kammbi, but attending the teachings with Morrim Goinz had opened my mind up to something bigger than myself and had strengthened my connection to Latisha. The fact that I received the book from Darcie had made me believe that it was meant to be here in Walter's Grove.

"It is an interesting declaration," the morrim continued. "A declaration that built this city. And how can an outsider like myself and the others that have come from Issabella, a city north of the Great Forest, object to it?"

Morrim Goinz held up the Book of Kammbi that lay on the podium in front of him in his thin, brittle-looking hands. The morrim had short, gray hair and wide eyes that took in everything around him as he taught. "These words in here tell me so. But I don't come just to tell you that every word in this book is in total disagreement with the Wall of Walter's Declaration. I love music. I love dance. I danced at parties back in Issabella all the time before I became a morrim. Movement is good physically but we need to do it by the spirit, in our case, the Eternal Comforter. Not for lust or desire out of its proper context. Everyone wants to love and be loved. But without a connection to something bigger than ourselves and a guide to navigate, the affairs of the heart can lead you astray. Our connection to Kammbi is what keeps us whole. Keeps us on balance and away from committing acts of passha. Keeps us in line with the one who gives life. The Life Giver wants all people from both regions of this land to be connected to him. And we have seen two men: one from the past and one from the present try to connect both regions for the glory of Kammbi. That's why we are here. And thanks to Brother Ciscoe Maldonado, we know the seeds have been planted."

The morrim smiled at me after his teaching. I nodded and replied, "People of the city believe in loving freely. Walter Fuente made that clear from his declaration, and everything in his life since he left the city of Terrance augmented that belief."

"Very good, Brother Ciscoe," Morrim Goinz said. "I have learned a lot from you since I arrived in this city. You speak of free love and I wonder… is love really free? For example, you have been married to Mrs. Maldonado for sixteen years, correct?"

I nodded.

"Alright, if love is free, as you say, would you mind if Sister Latisha gave it to another man as much as she has given it to you?"

I looked over at my wife and she frowned. I shook my head in disagreement.

"There you go, Brother Ciscoe. You don't want your wife to give her love to another man. Why is that?"

"She has been the one person I feel the most connected too. Her love for me has been genuine and I don't want to share it with another man."

Latisha smiled and caressed my right hand.

Morrim Goinz grinned and continued. "So then we have a flaw in Walter Fuente's declaration. I know his marital arrangement worked for him. But let me ask this question. If he believes in free love like he has declared, why stop with two wives? Why not three? Four? Or ten or twenty?"

I had to acknowledge Morrim Goinz's point. Love was never truly free. Conditions were always attached to love. I had learned that lesson from my wife in our marriage.

"Speaking of love, there is something I love to do just as much as I love my wife," I stated. "It is becoming clear that my love of Guanamamma music and dancing is being pushed out for another form of music."

Morrim Goinz stared off for a moment before he replied. I could feel the stares from the other parishioners in the Kahall. "I see, Brother Ciscoe. Why do you think Guanamamma music and dancing is being pushed out?"

"There is a belief that our music has been stolen from the native tribe of this area. Walter Fuente took the music of the Nerdann tribe and made it his own without giving them proper credit," Latisha added, before I could respond to his question.

I nodded and added. "That's a lie, Morrim Goinz. Our history is clear that Walter Fuente acknowledged his new musical style with the Nerdann tribe and had several tribe members in his band during his time. Why do people just ignore those facts and believe something else?"

Morrim Goinz grabbed The Book of Kammbi from the podium and stepped towards the parishioners. "Let's go to the book to see what Kammbi has to say about it. In Book Seven of the Ryianza section, Chapter Twelve, Kammbi says these words: *Truth will always find a way to present itself, even when untruth speaks louder. Untruth that sounds like the truth is deceptive and persuasive. But truth never has to shout or demand itself to be right amongst untruth.*"

"I've read those words from Chapter Twelve," I replied. "And that untruth is taking away something I love. I cannot let that happen."

I felt the stares from the other parishioners as Morrim Goinz returned behind the podium and continued reading. "*Never attempt to right a wrong with another wrong. People believe that getting even will right a wrong. However, it will lead down a path to self-destruction. And self-destruction is the quickest way to become disconnected from the ones you love and the one who loves us all. Let the Eternal Comforter guide you before you decide to right a wrong. Because life has a way of showing the proper outcome, even when you cannot see it in the moment.* Brother Ciscoe and Sister Latisha, I ask you as believers and followers of Kammbi not to engage in correcting a wrong with someone who wants to take away the thing you love to do. Trust the Eternal Comforter to guide your actions and words and let the wrongdoer be exposed for who they are."

***

Percy called me on the phone later that day. He wanted to apologize about having Ralph Johnson give me that letter. We had left The Tajara after our performance and Percy said that he should have kept us in his office so he could talk about it in person. He knew we went to Saahib's and had Ralph bring us the letter. I accepted his apology and explanation. I felt it was sincere and knew he was getting pressured from Darcie Fendlewiesen and Raphael Reynolds. He did not say that we were fired from performing at the nightclub. Percy would have to shelve our performance for the time being. I asked him if he was talking on the phone in his office to Darcie or Raphael after our performance. He went silent on the phone for a moment. I knew I had to confront them.

Latisha went to help Saahib out at the restaurant for the evening. I have always appreciated their relationship. Latisha admired her little brother and how he made something of himself with the restaurant. Saahib loved his big sister and was her biggest supporter, outside of me. I wished I had a sibling relationship like they had. However, I was the only child from my parents and I didn't remember them ever mentioning they wanted to have another child to go along with me as I grew up. I knew my father did not want to have any more children because it would have gotten in the way of his dancing.

Darcie's was the third and last Level One Nightclub in the Roxie and Penelope District. Darcie Fendlewiesen had always considered Darcie's the best Level One Nightclub in the district. We always enjoyed dancing at Darcie's the handful of times we visited. It was the largest of three Level One Nightclubs and had an elegant atmosphere that I liked. The club was three blocks away from the Mango on the corner of Ave Roxie and Ave Naima. Darcie's took the entire block and was always packed to capacity.

It took me about ten minutes to get into the nightclub. The entrance line went all the way out to Ave Naima but it moved quickly. I entered and walked down the main hallway that led to the dance floor in the east section of the nightclub. People were dancing to Piccanta music played over the sound system. The music had that same deep, drumbeat and people danced like they were having sex. I shook my head as I walked past the dance floor to the special section behind it.

"Mr. Ciscoe Maldonado has decided to make an appearance at my nightclub. To what do I owe your presence, sir?" Darcie said, as I arrived at her table. She was sitting with Raphael Reynolds and both had several drinks of javann liquor at their table.

Darcie had long, blond hair that went halfway down her back. She had small eyes but high cheekbones that gave an interesting facial structure. Darcie was not beautiful in a classic sense but striking. However, she knew how to attract attention with her penchant for wearing colorful tight skirts that showed off her wide hips. Darcie wore a lot of silver jewelry that dangled from her neck, wrist, and ears. The nightclub owner soaked attention from her patrons like a queen being honored by her subjects.

"Why did you pressure Antonio Henderson to get us fired from the Mango and have Percy Braxton give me a letter that wants us removed from The Festival of Josette?" I said, and sat down across from them.

Raphael Reynolds laughed and said, "The upholder of Guanamamma music and dancing has arrived. This is a special occasion indeed." He raised his glass of javann liquor at me.

"Where did you hear that from? Is your benefactor giving you bad information?" Darcie said, as a waitress handed me a glass of brownberry juice.

"Delia did not have to tell me what you are doing. The actions of your fellow Level One Nightclub owners have shown me what you are up to."

"You do catch on quickly," Raphael interjected, and continued with his drink of javann.

I watched my former lover take a sip of her drink. "I don't want to argue with the man that I first connected with in this city. You are a smart man, Ciscoe Maldonado. You should know why you and your lovely wife were removed from The Festival of Josette."

"What does Diondray Azur have to do with it?" I replied. "It has been four years since he was here in Walter's Grove."

Darcie frowned. "You showed him that book and confirmed for him that people in this city believed in those backwards teachings. Now we have morrims and diakonos in Walter's Grove. This city was never meant to hold believers or followers in that awful religion of Kammbi."

"I showed Diondray because he was questioning his belief about becoming the one to fulfill Oscar's Prophecy. Seeing The Book of Kammbi just confirmed there has always been a connection between both regions of Kammbia. And that belief in Kammbi existed here in our city. Remember you gave me that book."

Darcie frowned. "The worst decision I have ever made in my life. I should have burned that book!"

"It was a gift from your father."

"I did not know that, Darcie," Raphael said. "I still have a lot to learn about you."

Darcie went pale and looked away from Raphael. "Don't bring my past into this. You convinced Diondray that he should fulfill Oscar's Prophecy and now he is nowhere to be found."

I finished my glass of brownberry juice. "What are you talking about? I got a *themily* from him last year saying he had returned to Charlesville. He has been there since that letter."

Darcie turned back towards me and seemed to regain her composure. "No. His Uncle Xavier forced him to leave the city and no one knows where he is. Furthermore, I blame you for showing him that book. Since you took something from me, I must take something from you."

"You loved him," I replied. "I did not know you would be interested in a man almost half your age."

"You loved Diondray Azur?" Raphael said, and sat up straight in his seat. "How can you love a man who thinks he is the one to unite this entire land?"

"I think it is time for you to leave, Ciscoe," Darcie said.

"I'm going to dance at The Festival of Josette. You may have pressured the other Level One Nightclub owners into stopping Latisha and I from dancing at their nightclubs. But it will not work. And Guanamamma music and dancing is what this city was built on. That will never change."

Raphael curled his lips. "Guanamamma music was stolen from the original people of this area. It's time for the truth come out."

"Your truth, Raphael. Piccanta music is second rate and has nothing but drums. Real music is more than that!"

"Goodbye, Ciscoe. Thank you for coming tonight. But your time is up. You can always dance at those parties in the West Walter's Grove District. Those people will always appreciate stolen music," Darcie said curtly.

"Latisha and I are going to dance at The Festival of Josette whether you like it or not."

"That is out of your control, Ciscoe. Even Delia will not be able to help you. You took something from me and now it's time to return the favor."

I left the nightclub.

Chapter 5

We continued to practice our routine like we were going to perform at The Festival of Josette. There were only twenty-four days before the festival and I should have known that Darcie wanted to keep us from dancing there. We'd had our disagreements over the years about Guanamamma dancing. She believed that it should be danced freely and suggestively like Piccanta dancing. Of course, I did not. Our debate about Guanamamma dancing had lasted nearly twenty years. After our relationship ended, she vowed to get rid of Guanamamma dancing and now it seemed she was finally getting her wish fulfilled.

She knew Diondray was never going to stay in Walter's Grove. He had to travel to Terrance and back to his birth city of Charlesville to find out if he would fulfill the prophecy from The Book of Kammbi. Diondray felt he was chosen to fulfill that prophecy and the copy of the sacred book in our home confirmed he had to finish his journey. Darcie knew the prophecy better than me because she grew up with that religion when she lived in Santa Teresa. She should not have been surprised that he had to follow his destiny.

Darcie mentioned he had disappeared after returning to Charlesville. Where would he go? He was not coming back here. If she loved him as much as she apparently did, then she should to go

Charlesville and find him. Anyway, I had to push those thoughts aside as we practiced.

As dannzas, Latisha and I had developed a morning routine of a small breakfast, stretching, and practice for years. That routine helped in many ways, especially when life was not going our way. My father always told me that discipline and routine strengthen character, not stifle it. When bad things happened in life, having discipline would always come through for you, even when people did not. Latisha and I had a solid practice. We wanted to tighten our steps when we transitioned from the second point to the third point of the dance. I felt that transition was a little off when we performed at The Tajara. It had to be tighter for The Festival of Josette.

I played Natalia Havana's *My Night With You* as our practice song. Natalia Havana was known as the first lady of Guanamamma music and took the mantle after Walter Fuente died as the greatest singer in the city. Havana provided a woman's perspective as a counterbalance to Fuente's classic songs. She had a deep voice for a woman and her passionate singing style made it great for dancing. Natalia's voice lent itself to longer strides when we were dancing. Since Latisha was taller than myself, the strides felt in sync with her natural movement as a dancer. We decided after practice this would be the opening song for our dance at The Festival of Josette.

Latisha and I decided to go out to Club Hancock for the evening, since we did not have any nightclub performances. I was grateful that Latisha made sure we stayed on a budget and had savings that could sustain us for awhile. Also, Delia was working on getting house parties for us to dance at in the West Walter's Grove District. I was not enthused about doing those house parties. But we needed to keep dancing to stay sharp.

Club Hancock was a Level Two Nightclub on Ave Naima in the Roxie and Penelope District. It was a few blocks east of Darcie's. We had to drive by that nightclub in order to get to Club Hancock. I told Latisha about my meeting with Darcie and how she blamed me for showing Diondray The Book of Kammbi we had at the house. Also how Raphael continued to proclaim that Piccanta music was the city's true music.

Latisha disagreed with their explanations and wished she had gone with me as support. I did not want my wife with me when I met Darcie because the tension between those two women would have erupted. I wanted to hear from Darcie in her own words and alone.

We parked and entered Club Hancock. The nightclub was owned by Hancock Shorter and opened about a year before. I was trying to get Delia to arrange a meeting with him to see if Latisha and I could do our performance at the nightclub. But Delia said that Hancock felt he had to embrace Piccanta music and dancing to get patrons for the nightclub. However, he did like Guanamamma music and dancing. Hancock would find a way to make space at the club for Guanamamma music on occasion and tonight was one of those nights.

Club Hancock was a small nightclub about half the size of the Level One Clubs and got packed quickly. However, the crowd was light that night and maybe that's why Hancock wanted to have a Guanamamma music performance for the evening. The dance floor took up the middle section of the nightclub and seating went around it in a circular fashion.

A new singer named Zakiyah was starting to get attention around the city for her rendition of Guanamamma music. Zakiyah's voice made her in demand at the biggest house parties in the West Walter's Grove District. Delia told me she had performed for the major liquor owners like Maxwell Martinez of Maxwell Liquors, Casey Piccone of the Casey Company, and Bertha Bottomfelder of Bottomfelder Liquors at their houses. Also, she had just performed in the prior month of Aym, the fifth, at Civita member Katrina St. Clair's fiftieth birthday party. Zakiyah was in high demand in that district.

She was compared to Natalia Havana, the first lady of Guanamamma music. Zakiyah had sung her own versions of Havana's best songs like *My Night With You, These Tears Are Not For You, You Are So Much Better Than That,* and *I'm Moving On* that sounded just as good as the original versions. Latisha and I were looking forward to hearing her sing. We sat in the front row just to the right of the stage. I made sure we had a good seat for Zakiyah's performance.

"Welcome to Club Hancock!" the announcer said. He was a slim man wearing a black jumpsuit and a thin sliver necklace that dangled off his chest. "Hancock has a special treat for you all tonight. He has been trying to get this beautiful woman to perform here at Club Hancock since we opened our doors last year. Finally, she has agreed to sing for us tonight. I would like everyone to give a big and warm Club Hancock welcome to Zakiyah!"

The patrons applauded loudly as the spotlight appeared on the singer. Zakiyah was a heavy-set woman with a caramel-colored complexion. She wore a gold sequin maxi-length dress. Zakiyah looked great and her smile filled the room. She had a band behind her as they began the song.

My love is loaded
Like bullets in a gun
Waiting for the trigger
To be pulled
By the right man in my life

The guitarist began a solo after that first verse. However, I kept my eyes on Zakiyah. She continued to smile and swayed to the music.

Make sure you aim correctly
Because if you don't
It can cause damage
And end up hurting someone you did not love

The altophone horn player took his turn for a solo. Zakiyah faced him and he smiled at her before he played. He had a deep, wailing sound that fit the song.

"Give it up for Travis Navarro, the best altophone horn player in the city," Zakiyah announced. Travis was a tall, rail-thin man with a long black ponytail down his back. Everyone clapped for Travis and he played harder to the applause.

Hurts so deep
Making me feel like
I don't want to go on
You pulled the trigger
For my love
But I saw your affections
For another
Why did you pull the trigger?
If you did not want me?
Did she love you better than I could?
What did I do
To receive this kind of hurt

The timbau player created a soft, low sound as he held the drum between his legs. It reminded me of Natalia Havana's *These Tears Are Not For You*. That song was about a breakup in Havana's real life and she had laid it bare in the music. Zakiyah's song had a similar rhythm and I could tell she was influenced by Havana's song. I heard the pandretta player slap her hand against the percussion instrument. She was in sync with the timbau drum player and it had that Guanamamma feel. I was already thinking how Latisha and I would dance to Zakiyah's song. Despite the sadness of the song, I rocked back and forth in my seat. I looked at Latisha and she was doing the same. Zakiyah's voice was not as deep as Natalia's. But Zakiyah's passion was similar to that of her predecessor.

"We can dance to this song," Latisha said softly.

"I was thinking the same thing," I replied, and reached for her hand under the table.

My love is loaded
Like bullets in a gun
Waiting for the trigger
To be pulled
By the right man in my life
But don't come near
If you don't know
How to handle me
Because my love is loaded.

The band finished the song and we all gave them a standing ovation. Zakiyah smiled and blew kisses to the audience. Latisha and I looked at each other and knew we wanted to dance to Zakiyah's music. We gave a note to our server to pass along to Zakiyah. I hoped we could get a chance to meet her.

"Thank you Club Hancock for having us tonight," Zakiyah said after the standing ovation. "We have another song to do for you later. Let me introduce the rest of the band. Please give it up for Cheeky Gonzalez, the best timbau drummer in the city."

The crowd applauded as Cheeky smiled. His name suited him

perfectly. He was a fair complexioned man with prominent cheeks.

"Give it up for the baddest pandretta player in the city. And a sister in spirit, Gwendolyn Ruiz!" The crowd continued their applause for Gwendolyn as she blew kisses to them. My wife stood up for Gwendolyn and I noticed how similar they looked. Ruiz was more slender than Latisha, but their hairstyle, skin tone, and facial features reminded me of each other.

"Last but not least. The best guitar player in the city and one of the greatest songwriters I have ever come across in my career. Give it up for Franklin Fields. We always call him F Square."

The crowd applauded for F Square as he played several guitar licks to show his appreciation. He was a compact-built man with a coffee-colored complexion. F Square looked like he was meant to play guitar.

"Thank you, Zakiyah and the band," the announcer said, after returning to the stage. "We will see you later for another song. Now it's time to dance the evening away."

The sound system player came on and I heard *Don't Be Afraid To Shake What You Got* by Coltrain Hayes. I sighed. Coltrain Hayes had begun his long career singing Guanamamma music. He wrote songs about women he had relationships with like *Tameka, Anna, & Wanda.* They were declarations of love for him. But he decided to change to Piccanta music a couple years ago to stay relevant. I thought his newer songs were formulaic and a quick way to make some money.

"Are you Ciscoe Maldonado?"

A tan complexioned man wearing an orange jumpsuit and matching headdress approached our table.

"I am," I replied. "Do I know you from somewhere?"

The man extended his hand in greeting. He had a firm handshake. "I'm Ravi Gancha, owner of Gancha's in the Viddhana neighborhood of the South Walter's Grove District. Mrs. Delia Villanueva told me about your situation and I would like to see if you and your lovely wife want to dance at my house in a few days from now."

I looked over at Latisha and she smiled at Ravi's compliment.

"We are free these days and will accept your offer," I replied.

Ravi smiled and pulled out a card from his left pocket. "Here's my information and I want you both to come to my house tomorrow evening for a visit and we can talk further. I think the world of Mrs. Delia Villanueva and if she vouches for you, then I'm interested. Looking forward to seeing you tomorrow evening."

He gave Latisha a kiss on her right hand and walked away.

"I would have never thought that people from the Viddhana neighborhood would be interested in Guanamamma dancing," Latisha said.

"Same here," I added. "Delia has done it again."

***

Latisha and I got dressed the next evening to go to Ravi Gancha's home in the Viddhana neighborhood of the South Walter's Grove District. The neighborhood sat west of Ave Kummar, the city's longest street, and just south of Ave Guana, the street that created the border for the South Walter's Grove District.

The Viddhana people first settled in this part of city nearly one hundred years ago. Viddhana Hampi was the first explorer that came across the Omarra Sea into the western part of the land. I had always learned in school about the explorer Hendric Terrance Goltz who came across the Kammara Sea from the east, but not much about Viddhana Hampi. I learned about Viddhana Hampi and his people from Delia. Hampi left his homeland of Kanataka looking for silver. However, when the explorer and his small group of people arrived in the region they discovered guanna stalks instead of silver. Guanna stalks were a native plant to the region mostly in the area between the cities of Walter's Grove and Adrian. The plant had been cultivated for food and the liquor: javann. Disillusioned by the discovery of the guanna stalks, Viddhana Hampi wanted to return to Kanataka and begin another exploration to find silver. However, the people that came with him wanted to stay and make a life in this new land. Viddhana reluctantly agreed with his people and prayed to their god, Hoymala for a sign that they were meant to remain in this land. The sign came when some members of the Nerdann tribe showed the Viddhana people how to cultivate guanna stalks to make their own food. Hampi believed it was meant for his people to remain in the land and declared this section of Walter's Grove as the new homeland for the Viddhana people.

Ravi Gancha's home was a block east of where Ave Guana and Ave Chinnai intersected. Ave Chinnai was one of the two main roads for the Viddhana neighborhood. This street held the Viddhana Festival each year. Latisha and I came to the festival five years before and it was the most colorful and extravagant festival we had ever seen. It was one of the few occasions that the neighborhood opened itself to the rest of the city. We were looking forward to attending the Viddhana Festival that following year, but the Civita created a law prohibiting non-residents of the Viddhana neighborhood from attending the festival. There was a belief that the Viddhana Festival would upstage The Festival of Josette as the city's main festival. The Civita got pressured by the Regnator and the wealthy citizens of West Walter's Grove District to create the law. It was an awful thing to do and Delia had tried to get it changed since it was enacted.

The home was in a hastancia style similar to what you would see in the city of Adrian. The hastancia homes were wide, flat, two-story buildings that resided on a couple of acres each in the neighborhood.

The Viddhana people had large families and preferred this style of home over the Bremen style that was in the rest of Walter's Grove. I immediately noticed the huge malpe trees that towered the property from the rear. Those malpe trees were a signature feature of every hastancia home I had ever seen. The main walkway created a straight path through spectacular grounds. I could smell the perfectly cut grass with orange, white, and silver flowers on each side along with small brownberry trees. The home was decorated in orange and silver, the main colors of the Viddhana people. Two men at the main entrance greeted us. They wore orange jumpsuits and matching headdresses. Silver necklaces, bracelets, and belts accessorized the jumpsuits. The man on the left side of the entrance opened the door and we entered the home.

The living room was enormous and had a dance floor where three women were dancing to a fast drumbeat. The women were known as Lavanny dancers. Lavanny was a traditional dance of the Viddhana people. I understood from the Viddhana Festival we attended that this part of the dance was meant to be received as an invitation. Latisha and I watched the Lavanny dancers move across the dance floor in a movement similar to a side step in Guanamamma dancing. The Lavanny dancers were dressed in orange maxi dresses accentuated with silver on the sleeves, midsection, and the bottom of the dress. Each woman wore a thick silver necklace with a large orange pendant. The Lavanny dancers looked beautiful.

Ravi Gancha greeted us a few minutes after the invitation dance. He had a big smile on his face and motioned us to a table just past the dance floor. The table was decorated in orange and silver and filled with food. There were several people sitting at the table waiting for us to be seated.

"I'm delighted you have decided to take up my invitation for this evening," Ravi said, as we took our seats. "I could tell you both enjoyed the invitation dance from our Lavanny dancers. We always welcome friends with that dance."

"The dance was similar to a dance step we use in Guanamamma dancing," Latisha said. "I liked the way the Lavanny dancers glided across the floor with that side step."

Ravi placed his hand in front of his face and tilted his head forward. "Thank you, Mrs. Latisha, for your observation. Our style of dancing is quite similar to Guanamamma dancing. That's why I wanted to invite you to my home. However, we will get to that discussion later. The Viddhana people do not like to discuss business before dinner."

I met his family while a couple of servers began placing food on our plates and filling our glasses with drink. Ravi sat in between his sister, Anil, to the left of him, and his mother, Saloni, to the right of him. To the left of Anil were her husband, Tarique and their two daughters, Kamanda and Bismilla.

"Thank you for coming, Mr. Ciscoe and Mrs. Latisha," Bismilla said, after she gave us a big smile. "I told my uncle that Parvah and I appreciated how much you both stood up for us at your teaching session. We did not think that other people in the city would have made that kind of gesture for our people."

"Our teaching sessions are for anyone who wants to learn Guanamamma dancing," Latisha added. "My husband and I will not tolerate anyone being treated like they don't belong in our class."

I nodded in agreement as the entire family at the dinner table gave us warm smiles of approval.

"Please bow your heads," Saloni said softly. Ravi's mother had an angular facial structure with high cheekbones. Her complexion was a shade darker than her children and it made me wonder what their father looked like. Saloni led a prayer, blessing the food, family, and guests that would partake at dinner. The prayer was short but meaningful.

"How long have you both been dancing?" Ravi asked, after several minutes into the dinner. I had just bitten into a piece of Apma, a triangular-shaped sweet flat bread with a honey spread on top. It was so soft that it melted in my mouth. I remembered having Apma at the Viddhana Festival and could not stop eating it.

"We've been married for sixteen years and started dancing together a year prior," Latisha answered. "I knew Ciscoe would only marry someone that could dance with him. I wanted to make sure that would be me."

Everyone laughed at the table. I patted Latisha's thigh and she smiled at me. I don't remember ever demanding that she had to dance. But she assumed correctly that I would want a wife who could dance Guanamamma.

"Hopefully Ravi can find someone that he can come together with, like you two," Saloni interjected. Ravi rolled his eyes. "We are looking forward to seeing you dance in a few nights here. The Viddhana people love Guanamamma dancing and it has a similarity to Lavanny dancing."

Ravi sighed and added, "Please excuse my mother. She is always trying to find me a wife. But she is correct in the fact that there are similarities between the dances. And we feel if we can have expert Guanamamma dancers showcased in our neighborhood on a regular basis, then it will give us a connection to the rest of the city."

"As you know, Guanamamma dancing is being pushed out for Piccanta dancing. Latisha and I have lost our jobs in the Roxie and Penelope District and the people of the city seem to not appreciate Guanamamma music and dancing anymore."

Ravi frowned. "Yes, Mr. Ciscoe. Delia told me what has happened with your situation. That's why I reached out to you both. I believe our connection can help each of us. We would like more people from the other districts to come to the neighborhood to enjoy our food, listen to our music, and be a part of the Viddhana Festival. The Viddhana neighborhood wants to be a part of this city."

I nodded. "This neighborhood is a part of our city. I'm sad that we are not allowed to attend the Viddhana Festival anymore. I hope that awful law gets changed."

"I appreciate your sentiment, Mr. Ciscoe," Anil answered. I noticed she had the same tan complexion and facial features as her brother. But her dark brown eyes were the most prominent facial feature and they could draw you in easily. "My brother has been working with Mrs. Delia Villanueva for quite some time to get that law removed. But their efforts have not made the Civita or the Regnator budge. We want to show that the Viddhana people are no different than any other people in this city. And if we can connect through dance, maybe that will open the eyes of the rest of the city that we all are one people."

"Plus I like Mrs. Delia for my son!" Saloni added.

Everyone laughed again at the table. I saw Ravi blush and got a sense that he did have feelings for Delia. Was Delia going to talk to me about that as well?

"We have another performance for you to watch," Ravi said.

I nodded while eating Maharra, a spicy rice based dish with grilled chicken and yellow peas. I dipped the Apma into the bowl of Maharra and it was delicious. I had to add this Viddhana food to our regular dinners.

After dinner, we returned to the dance floor and sat on a royal blue sofa. The dance floor lighting dimmed and a spotlight appeared in the center of the room. There stood a man dressed in a light orange jumpsuit with silver and orange jewelry on his neck and wrists. The man held a drum that was strapped over his left shoulder.

"Viddhana!" the man bellowed.

Four new Lavanny female dancers each dressed in a silver sari appeared behind the drummer. They stood in a square formation with plenty of space between them. I noticed the sari had orange jewelry around the waist and at the bottom. Their silver headdresses had an orange stone in the center. These women looked elegant.

The drummer began the performance with a slow drum roll. The dancers raised their arms above their heads and dropped them suddenly to the beat. They moved three steps to the right and then three steps to the left in perfect coordination. Next, the dancers moved counterclockwise as the drumming got faster. Meanwhile, their arms waved like a bird's wings.

Boom!

Latisha looked at me as a loud sound like a bomb went off. I searched around to see where it was coming from. Ravi's family was transfixed on the drummer and dancers. They knew the bomb was a part of the performance.

I turned back in my seat and saw four male dancers had appeared next to the female dancers. The male dancers wore silver jumpsuits with orange necklaces. They created pairs and danced together while the drummer returned to a slower drum roll. The spotlight appeared again to the right of everyone. There was a tall woman dressed like the female dancers that came into view. She held an altophone horn and began to play softly.

The paired dancers faced each other and moved in a back-and-forth step similar to how Latisha and I danced. However, the dancers did not touch or hold each other. The male dancers led the movement and the female dancers followed. Latisha gaped at me as they moved from a back-and-forth step into a sidestep position. This performance had incorporated more elements of Guanamamma dancing. I could not believe what I was seeing.

"Viddhana!" the drummer bellowed again.

The horn player continued as the drummer stopped playing. The paired dancers formed a line and waved their arms in sync to the horn sound. They exited the dance floor to the right in a single file. The spotlight gleamed on each dancer as they bowed to us.

We are all connected. If there's anything I have learned from traveling in both regions of this land, Ciscoe, we are all connected. And the sooner we can realize it, the better off we will be as people.

Diondray's words from his last letter came to mind. We were all connected.

"That was fantastic, Ravi!" Latisha said as we returned to the dinner table for drinks and dessert.

Ravi smiled. "I noticed your reaction throughout this second part of the dance. It is called the acceptance of the invitation."

"That was Guanamamma dancing," I interjected. "I would have never thought the Viddhana people would include elements of Guanamamma dancing into their performance."

"We always used those elements in our dancing. We as Viddhana people have always loved Guanamamma music and dancing, even though we came to this land nearly one hundred years ago. In all of the establishments here in the neighborhood, we play that type of music along with our Viddhana music," Anil added.

"Our family would like you to perform at our establishment, Gancha's, once every seven days. If you have a band, we can accommodate them too. I believe your dancing is still needed in this city. And our neighborhood will support you," Ravi said.

I smiled and shook hands with Ravi. Saloni said another prayer after our handshake and it felt like a blessing.

Chapter 6

Before we danced at Gancha's, Delia got us work at a house party in West Walter's Grove. Bertha Bottomfelder of Bottomfelder Liquors requested that Latisha and I dance at her home for one of her regular weekly parties. I was dreading this opportunity. It made me remember those house parties my father danced at during my childhood and I never felt that I belonged amongst those people. There was a lot of javann drinking, partner swapping, and talking down about the other districts of the city. I used to overhear some of the wealthiest people of the city tell my father that he should move from East Walter's Grove District and not associate with the common folk. He was an exceptional dancer and greatness belonged with the best people of the city.

"We have to keep dancing, my love," Latisha said, as I entered the gate to Bertha's home. "Remember we danced at these house parties before we got to dance at the nightclubs in the Roxie and Penelope District."

"I know, my love. But these people don't care about anyone in the rest of the city and they look down on us," I replied, as I parked the automobile.

"I know the stories you've told me about when your father danced at these parties. He made a lot of money and that money got the house he left us. Many of these people really appreciated your father's dancing and it has created an opportunity for us to do the same."

I sighed and reached for my wife's hand. "You have always been more the practical one, my love. Let's give them our best." I kissed her hand and we got out of the automobile.

Bertha Bottomfelder's home was in a classic Bremen style with the top part decorated in a diamond shaped pattern surrounding two windows. She had diamond-shaped ornaments hanging from the outside window ledges and I had to admit that it looked stylish. It seemed that Bertha loved her diamonds.

"Ciscoe and Latisha Maldonado!" Bertha said, as we entered the home. She had a big smile on her face and hugged both of us. "Thank you for coming to my home. Delia told me what happened with those second rate nightclubs in the Roxie and Penelope District. That's too bad. You don't need to be with those people anyway. They don't know how to appreciate the music and dancing that created the city. We sure do here in the district and your father, Gustavoe, understood that."

I glanced at Latisha and saw her lips form *It's okay.* I nodded as we followed Bertha further into the home. Bertha Bottomfelder was a full-figured woman and dressed in a black maxi dress that seemed to be a couple sizes smaller than her normal size. She had diamond-shaped silver necklaces and bracelets dangling from her neck and wrists. Bertha moved through the house gracefully and every partygoer raised their glass of Bertha's javann liquor as we passed them.

"You will be dancing here," Bertha stated, as we reached the back of the house and stood on the patio. "I'm glad it's a clear night for both of you. I have a talented singer that will be the music for your performance."

"Delia did not tell us we would be dancing with a singer," I added curtly.

"Don't worry, Ciscoe. The singer I have chosen for tonight knows this music very well," Bertha replied, and squeezed my right shoulder.

I was dreading this already. I never danced with a singer I had not practiced with beforehand. I had to learn how a singer phrased the lyrics of the song they sung. I had to learn their voice and made sure our steps were in sync. We were going blind into the performance. Not good.

"I will return shortly with the singer," Bertha said, and squeezed my shoulder again. "If the people love your dancing tonight, I would like to have you both as the regular performance for my parties. I will pay you double what you were getting at those nightclubs."

"Thank you for your offer. Ciscoe and I will consider it."

I was glad that Latisha spoke at that moment. Everything in me wanted to reject Bertha's offer, even though the money would be twice what we got from Antonio and Percy.

"Focus, my love," Latisha said, after Bertha left the patio. "I need you thinking about the dance. We will dance to the song and make our money. We can do that, my love."

"Ciscoe and Latisha, I'm so glad it is you who will be dancing to our music tonight."

I was getting ready to reply to Latisha's encouragement when Zakiyah spoke to us. She had a look of relief on her face. I was surprised to see her.

"Bertha did not tell us until we arrived that a couple would be dancing to our first song," the singer continued, as the band began setting up on the patio. "We never had anyone dance to our music and to get Mr. and Mrs. Maldonado for our first time is better than I expected when we accepted this job."

"We are glad that it is you," I replied. "My wife and I saw your performance at Club Hancock and we were thinking how we could dance to that song."

"Dancing to *My Love is Loaded,*" Zakiyah said. "Wow, that's one of the saddest songs I have ever written. I did not think anyone would ever want to dance to it."

"That song reminds us of Natalia Havana's *These Tears Are Not For You,*" Latisha added.

"My favorite Natalia song," Zakiyah interjected. "*My Love is Loaded* was influenced by that song. Natalia is our greatest Guanamamma singer, even more so than Walter Fuente. Her music touches you deep and I hope to do that with my music."

Bertha returned with the partygoers and directed them to sit at the tables that were placed on the lawn across from the patio.

"You have already met Zakiyah," Bertha said as she joined us. Zakiyah excused herself and went over to the band. "This is going to be a great party. Bertha Bottomfelder does it again!"

"We are glad that you got Zakiyah as the singer," I said with as much enthusiasm as I could muster. "She is carrying on the tradition of Guanamamma music these days and her presence on the scene is much welcomed."

Bertha placed her hand on my shoulder and replied, "The woman can sing. You both can dance. The audience will respond to the performance. Don't worry, Ciscoe. You will always have a place in this district."

She walked back to the partygoers that were seated across the patio. Latisha and I walked over to Zakiyah and she gave us a quick rundown of the first song they were going to sing. The lyrics reminded me of *My Love Is Loaded* and the band played some of the music briefly. It was up-tempo and had some swing to it. But it was definitely a Guanamamma song and however I felt about being here started to melt away.

I won't be denied
I won't be deterred
I only think of you
Can't you see that I love you?

Zakiyah sang that first verse without the band and with such passion that she had the audience in the palm of her hand instantly. We began our dance once the music came on afterwards. F Square started the music with his guitar.

We made it through the first point of the dance as Travis created a wah-wah sound on the altophone horn. That sound blended with F Square's playing. Latisha and I did a few extra back-and-forth steps before we went to the second point of the dance. I would usually twirl my wife after four back-and-forth steps but the music lingered longer than usual for a Guanamamma song.

Don't you understand
I need your comfort
I need your touch
I need your pleasure
Don't you understand
I need you

Zakiyah sang the second verse as we made it to the second point of the dance. I moved Latisha into some side steps and finally twirled her a couple times. She squeezed my left hand tighter than usual and whispered, "Hold me closer."

I was surprised by the request, but I had no time to object because the pandretta percussion player finally brought her instrument into the song. I felt Latisha's body closer than usual and had no time to adjust my body.

The altophone horn joined his bandmates with the same sound from earlier. I returned to the back-and-forth step as we began the third point of the dance.

"Let's move together in a circle."

"We have no time for that," I whispered back to Latisha.

"Let's do it anyway."

I nodded and pressed my guide hand closer on her back and moved her to the left. We circled around a couple times as the timbau drum and pandretta percussion played faster.

"Another circle."

I repeated the step and heard a loud applause from the crowd. People were standing and clapping harder as we did another circle step. I had not seen an audience react like that in a long time.

You can't deny
My love for you
You can't deny
My love is real
You can't deny
That I'm always
Here for you
You can't deny
I'm all the woman
You will ever need
You can't deny it

Zakiyah sang the final verse of the song after the audience returned to their seats. Latisha and I made it to the third point of the dance. My wife had an excited look on her face I had not seen since we first started dancing. I felt out of sorts because we deviated from our usual routine. The audience loved it. The song was great.

However, I did not feel it like everyone else.

"Thank you, Zakiyah, the band, and the great dancing from Ciscoe and Latisha Maldonado!" Bertha announced after the performance. "We love Guanamamma music and dancing here. And we just had a performance for the ages!"

The audience rose from their seats and gave us a standing ovation. Latisha and I did our customary bow. I walked away from the patio and headed into the house by myself.

"Did I do something wrong?" Bertha said, as she came into the living room where I was sitting.

Latisha was sitting next to me and squeezed my hand. "My husband did not want to dance here tonight. He did this for me."

I took several deep breaths to regain my composure. Why could I not get that reception at the nightclubs? We danced the same way besides turning in circles for the past year and the patrons at the Mango and The Tajara rejected it. I wanted those people to react the way the people at this house party did.

"I'm sorry, Ciscoe," Bertha said, as she sat down on the other side of me. "I want to have a great house party and ensure all my guests enjoy themselves. It saddens me that you feel bad after such a wonderful performance. My partygoers loved it."

I looked at Bertha and saw a genuine look of concern on her face. "I appreciate you giving Latisha and I this opportunity to dance at your home. My wife is right that I did not want to dance here this evening. I did it for her. I wanted that kind of applause from the people that go to the Roxie and Penelope District. Not here."

Bertha patted my thigh. "Oh, I get it. Guanamamma dancing is meant for everyone, not just people of this district. That's a noble sentiment, Ciscoe. Delia told me that your father felt the same way. As you see, those people have rejected Guanamamma music and dancing. They feel it's from the past and time for something new.

You cannot stop people from feeling that way. Sometimes people just want something different and anything that reminds them of the past or tradition gets pushed aside."

"This city was created from Walter Fuente's music and dance," I said with anger in my voice. "Now the people of the city believe he stole this music from the original tribe of this area. How could they believe something like that?"

Latisha continued to squeeze and caress my hand. I wanted to leave Bertha's house at that moment and be alone with my thoughts.

"I don't believe Walter Fuente stole his music from Nerdann tribe," Bertha replied. "I've heard those kinds of comments for years. Those people have always felt they were not a part of this city and decided as people to live outside it. They made their decision and it was not because Walter Fuente stole their music."

"Why do people believe a lie so easily?"

"Ciscoe, you should know that a lie always travels faster than the truth. I'm afraid you will have to let those people go and embrace the ones who still appreciate Guanamamma music and dancing. As I said earlier, you will have a place here in this district. The sooner you can accept this, the better you will be. Don't make the same mistake as your father," Bertha retorted.

"I'm ready to leave," I replied and got up from the sofa.

"That's unfortunate you are feeling the way that you do," Bertha replied, as she stood up as well. "But you and Latisha have an open invitation to dance here at my parties. I hope you accept it. Go where you are loved and leave those who have rejected you behind."

***

Delia arranged a meeting with the surviving members of the Nerdann tribe a few days later. There were only seventeen days before The Festival of Josette. We hoped this meeting would help us to remain at the festival and get the truth about Walter's relationship to them.

The Nerdann tribe lived fifteen minutes southeast of the city. The designated area was granted years ago to the tribe in order to preserve their way of life. Walter Fuente's arrival to this area brought many positive changes like the music, dance, and a city. However, there was a downside and the Nerdann tribe's way of life got pushed out as the city grew. Raphael Reynolds had made that point numerous times with his speeches at the Wall of Walter's Declaration. I agreed with him on that point but to declare that Walter Fuente stole the tribe's music went too far.

A man named Hannar greeted us. He was one of the elders of the tribe and the person Delia contacted to arrange our meeting. Hannar was of medium-height, lean, and had reddish-brown skin. His hair was cut in a bowl shape and he had a clean-shaven face.

"Welcome, Ciscoe and Latisha," Hannar said as he shook our hands. "We don't get many visitors from the city. It's nice to have some of the city folk come out to see us."

We followed Hannar past several triangular-shaped, mud-built homes in the center of the designated area. I had learned in school these homes were first built in the city before the Bremen-style homes became popular. They looked half the size of a Bremen-style home but just as decorative on the outside.

"Why is it that you don't get many visitors from the city?" Latisha asked.

Hannar stopped walking and faced us. "The city folk would like us to remain invisible. Help the businesses harvest the guanna stalks, brownberries, and corn. But stay on this land the great Walter Fuente gave us many years ago. And everything will be fine."

"Walter wanted you to have this land in order to keep your traditions. Was he wrong to give you this land?" I asked.

"The great Walter Fuente was not wrong in giving our people this land. The city started growing with people," Hannar explained. "Many of them came from his birth city of Terrance to the east. And quite a few of our people wanted to live in the city that he created from music and dance. He saw that our way of life would die out soon and felt responsible for it. His gift was an offering to offset it."

"At least he acknowledged what was happening at the time and tried to make amends," Latisha added.

"Yes, he did. And those of us who remain out here are appreciative of that gesture."

Hannar's explanation made me feel better about their relationship with Walter. His gift of this land might have seemed as a token to what his arrival in the area caused. He knew without the tribe's contribution, Walter's Grove could not have existed.

Hannar led us into a house where the other tribe members were sitting at a long table. They were three men and two women sitting across from each other. They rose from the chairs and Hannar bowed to them. Then he spoke in the Nerdann dialect that I could not understand. It sounded like a chant and lasted a couple of minutes.

We took our seats on the opposite end of the table from the elders. Hannar sat the closest to us and continued, "We appreciate your visit and desire to learn more about Walter Fuente's relationship to our people."

"That's correct, Hannar," I said. "My wife and I are dannzas. We danced to Guanamamma music in the nightclubs of the Roxie and Penelope District. However, it seems the people of the city want to move on from Guanamamma music for a new type of music called Piccanta. And one of the main proponents of this new music has been that the reason the city needs to move on from Guanamamma music is that Walter Fuente stole his musical style from your people. He had tribe members in his band recently making that accusation."

Hannar cut his eyes to the rest of the elders before answering.

They all had slight smiles on their faces. I sensed they would all be on the same page in the answer that Hannar would give us.

"Stolen from us," Hannar started. "No, the great Walter Fuente did not steal our music to create Guanamamma music. Our ancestors willingly shared our instruments, the timbau drum and pandretta percussion with him. He incorporated them into his musical style that he brought from the east. Our tribe has never accused the great Walter Fuente of stealing our music. How could one steal something that never belonged to him in the first place?"

I saw the rest of the elders nod in agreement at his comment.

"People of the city are believing he did steal his music from your people," Latisha said. "And because of it, my husband and I have lost our jobs as dannzas in the Roxie and Penelope District. Also, we are being kept from performing at The Festival of Josette. They are determined to get rid of Guanamamma music and dancing from the city for good."

"The new will always replace the old," Hannar replied. "That is how the cycle goes. The old wants to hold on for the sake of tradition. The new wants to push out the old for the sake of progress. And it seems that Guanamamma music and dancing have reached that point in the cycle."

The elders nodded once again.

"So you believe that Guanamamma music and dancing must be replaced by Piccanta music?" I asked.

Hannar looked at the elders again before answering. "The cycle always supersedes our personal feelings or connection to something. You cannot reverse the cycle or will you upset the balance of how life should go."

I sighed. "Guanamamma music means a lot to me, more than anything outside of my wife. I don't believe this music should be pushed aside from something new based on a falsehood. I will admit that it would be hard to accept the music being pushed aside in the proper way as you stated with the life cycle. However, I can not stand by and let a lie dictate the music that helped create a city."

One of the women elders gave me a warm smile after my comment. She motioned to Hannar and he joined them at their end of the table. They started chanting again and I looked at Latisha.

"Valencia senses your sincerity to the music and dance, and believes your point that it should not be pushed aside because of a falsehood. As I stated earlier, the great Walter Fuente did not steal our music. Valencia wants to help your cause. It is not the time in the cycle for the passing of Guanamamma music and dance. We have something to show you upon your next visit," Hannar said as he returned to our end of the table.

"Next visit!" I shot back. "I would like you to show us now."

Hannar gave a slight chuckle. "City folk have no patience. It is not the time to show you. The Nerdann tribe always honors the timing in everything. You will be shown what you need to see when you return."

I had not planned on returning out there. I wanted proof that Walter Fuente did not steal the tribe's music to show everyone in the city. The truth needed to be shown.

"You have an energy of anger and are not ready to receive what you need to see," Hannar said, after speaking with the other elders once again. "We believe you will have the correct energy when you return for your next visit."

The elders rose from their seats and shook our hands as we were leaving. *We are all connected. We just have to find the thing that connects us together.* Diondray's words came to mind once again. We were connected and that truth must be honored despite my frustration.

Chapter 7

I was nervous as we got ready to dance at Gancha's for the first time. Latisha and I dressed in our traditional black and silver dannza outfits. I wanted us to look our best and give the Viddhana audience the best presentation of ourselves.

"They will love our dancing," Latisha said in the waiting room of Gancha's. "The Lavanny dancers have incorporated elements of Guanamamma dancing into their routines. The audience knows the music. All we have to do is dance the way we always do."

I grabbed my wife's hands and kissed them gently. "You are correct, my love. I just have this nervous energy. I hope the audience loves our dancing. I need them to. It seems that the thing I love the most besides you is being taken away. That cannot happen, my love. It just can't."

Latisha smiled. "It will not happen. You will not let it happen. I will not let it happen. Delia will not let it happen. And we have a chance for a new audience tonight. They will not let it happen. So let's focus on that, my favorite short man, and dance like we know how."

Latisha and I embraced and held each other for a few moments. I needed that reassurance. She has always been the encourager in our marriage. I was grateful to have found someone like Latisha and remain monogamous to her for all of those years. She was truly my partner in every sense of that word.

***

"We have a special performance tonight," Ravi Gancha said to the audience. "Gancha's will be the first establishment in the Viddhana neighborhood to allow a dance performance from someone outside of the neighborhood. As my friend, Mrs. Delia Villanueva, has said often to the leaders of this neighborhood, Viddhana people are citizens of Walter's Grove. We belong to this city and it's time to be welcomed into the family."

I saw Delia smile from her seat in the audience. She was sitting in the center section right in front of the stage where Ravi was speaking. They were smitten with each other. Ravi glanced at her and smiled back. I was still surprised that Viddhana people would be interested in someone from outside of the neighborhood. Love can bring people together just like music and dancing.

"Please give a warm welcome to Ciscoe and Latisha Maldonado."

The audience clapped as I followed my wife onto the stage. Delia blew kisses at us. I noticed smiles from everyone in the audience. In the right section, I saw the Lavanny dancers from the performance at Ravi's house as well. It felt good to get this kind of reception.

"Viddhana!" one of the Lavanny musicians on the right side of the stage yelled.

We wanted to use the Lavanny musicians for our performance that night. Latisha and I had spent the last couple of days working with the Lavanny musicians for our performance. I had brought a selection of Guanamamma music that we danced in our practices. The musicians knew the songs from Walter Fuente, Natalia Havana, and John Jose Rollins. After our first practice, they came up with the music for that night's performance.

I glanced at the audience one last time before the music started. We had their attention. One of the musicians slapped the timbau drum as I led Latisha in the back-and-forth step. We moved four times in the basic Guanamamma step with the timbau drum. It sounded deep and solemn. He slapped the drum repeatedly as the altophone horn player joined him. The horn sound was tight with short bursts. It sounded a little off at first, but I could tell they were playing Guanamamma music. The Lavanny musicians were behind us on stage. Even though we were going to dance in a triangle, I had to be mindful of where the musicians were.

I twirled Latisha a couple of times after we made it to the second point of the dance. Another Lavanny musician with a pandretta joined the song. He shook the pandretta creating a chime-like sound that fell in sync with the other Lavanny musicians. I wanted to make sure I concentrated on how the musicians played. Even though the Lavanny musicians caught onto the songs I played during practice quickly, we'd only had two days together to get the performance correct. And this was the first song we had danced to without words in quite some time. The Lavanny musicians incorporated John Jose Rollins' song, *Can This Last Forever* for our performance. Rollins came on the scene about fifteen years before and many people in the city thought he would become the next Walter Fuente. But he only had that one hit song in his career and disappeared quickly. In practice, I saw how the musicians took to Rollins' song and I knew they were going to use it for that night.

Latisha gave her customary smile to let me know we were dancing well. I returned us to the basic Guanamamma step as we made our way to the third point of the dance. The audience began clapping to the music and I noticed people nodding their heads. I glanced at the musicians and the timbau player smiled at me.

We finished the dance with Latisha twirling multiple times and going into a sidestep position.

"Viddhana!"

We walked up to the edge of the stage and bowed. The audience rose from their seats and clapped loudly.

"Thank you, Ciscoe and Latisha Maldonado!" Ravi announced as we began to walk off the stage. "We are honored that you chose to dance at Gancha's tonight. May this become the first of many great dance performances here."

Latisha and I embraced. I did not know if the performance would help our chances in getting to perform at The Festival of Josette. But I could sense that something different had just happened and we were going to be a part of it.

After we changed into our regular clothing, we sat down at the table with Delia. Dinner had already been prepared for us. I was hungry and ready for some Maharra and Apma bread. However, there were several pieces of Apma bread with a combination of food items I had seen mixed together before.

"Mrs. Delia told me how much you love tortas," Ravi Gancha said as he joined us at the table. "Our people make a similar dish called Sassanna. It has brownberries, corn, grilled fish, and brown rice laid on a piece of Apma bread. I hope you like it."

"He will!" Latisha interjected.

Everyone at the table laughed as I took my first bite of Sassanna. It was excellent. The sweetness from brownberries complimented the fish, corn, and brown rice. Saahib's tortas had some competition. A waiter brought a second plate of Sassanna for me a few minutes later.

"Your dancing went perfectly with the music," Ravi said. "The musicians were glad that you brought music from John Jose Rollins to learn from. I've heard them play that song here at Gancha's quite often."

"I knew the musicians were going to choose John Jose Rollins' song after they heard it at practice," I replied. "Latisha and I had not danced to just music in a long time. We were pleased with the Lavanny musicians' version of the song."

"The roots of Viddhana music are similar to Guanamamma music," Ravi continued. "The use of the timbau drum, pandretta, and altophone horn is foundational to our music."

No wonder the Lavanny musicians caught on to those songs I played them at practice. Viddhana music used the same instruments and song structure as Guanamamma music. I wanted to listen to some of their music and learn how to dance to it. I knew we had to get the Lavanny musicians to perform at the Festival of Josette. They had a connection to our city's music and I wanted it to be shown to everyone.

"I loved that John Jose Rollins song," Delia added and smiled at Ravi. "I'm glad it was chosen for the performance. I believe it made an impression on everyone in the audience."

Latisha nodded. "Ciscoe and I would love to have a copy of that version of the song."

"We can get that for you by the end of the night. We record every performance on audio tape for the musicians to have," Ravi answered. "Mrs. Delia mentioned the impression the song made on everyone. We had several members of the Civita in the audience tonight. Haines Fonseca and his companion, Charlene, is sitting two tables behind us on the right. Also, we have Katrina St. Claire and her companion, Charles, sitting at the table to the left of them. Thanks to Mrs. Delia, they were able to come tonight. And the fact that you danced with the Lavanny musicians playing Guanamamma music shows how it can bring people together."

I turned around to see the Civita members sitting at the tables that Ravi mentioned. I did not realize that members of Civita were in the audience. Haines and Charlene waved at our table. So did

Katrina St. Claire and her companion. Delia waved back. I hoped that was a good sign.

"I had to make sure we got some members of the Civita here tonight," Delia said. "If they could see you and Latisha dance with the Lavanny musicians, then it can show how Guanamamma music is for everyone."

Latisha remarked, "If this was stolen music, then it could not be for everyone?"

"Right," Delia interjected. "Raphael Reynolds made his petition to the Civita to get Guanamamma music removed from The Festival of Josette on the basis that Walter Fuente stole it from the Nerdann tribe and excluded them as Walter's Grove became a city."

"But showing that the Lavanny musicians have always used the same instruments for their music reveals it could not have been stolen?" I replied.

"These instruments have been a part of our music since we arrived in this region of the land. Our ancestors came here many years after Walter Fuente did," Ravi said. "What you did with this evening's performance is so important. The Civita members just saw with their own eyes the blending of Viddhana music and Guanamamma dancing. Mr. Fonseca and Ms. St. Claire can talk with the other members of the Civita about this performance. This is the opportunity we have been asking for."

"That was a wonderful performance!" Katrina St. Claire said, as she came to our table and stood next to Delia.

"Thank you, Civita Member St. Claire," I said.

"Call me Katrina," she replied and smiled. "I'm not on duty. I'm just Katrina in this type of setting."

"We are glad you liked the performance," Delia said. "It shows how connected the Viddhana people are to the city."

Katrina nodded. "Noted, my friend. We will talk more about that later. But, you know the people want to hear Piccanta music these days. Guanamamma music is seen as something from the past and has a stigma associated with it."

"A stigma made from a falsehood," I fired back. "I would think a Civita member would know the truth about our music. It is chronicled in the building you work at."

Katrina frowned. "I did not come here tonight to be lectured about what a Civita member should know. However, I do know about Raphael Reynolds' petition to get Guanamamma music removed from The Festival of Josette."

"My husband and I have been removed from dancing at the Level One Nightclubs in the Roxie and Penelope District. We believe nightclub owner, Darcie Fendlewiesen has used her association with Raphael Reynolds to influence the other Level One Nightclub owners. Now she is trying to keep us from dancing at The Festival of Josette because of his petition."

Katrina glared at my wife.

"It's true, my friend," Delia replied.

"That is a serious accusation. You will need foolproof evidence before I could bring something like that to the other Civita members."

"That's why I wanted to have Ciscoe and Latisha dance with our musicians at my restaurant," Ravi added. "Our people have used the same instruments for our music as Guanamamma music. Their dancing blended naturally with our music. We hope to show that Raphael Reynolds's petition has no merit and should be removed immediately."

Katrina nodded at Ravi's comments. I could sense she had not known about the Viddhana people's connection to Guanamamma music before tonight.

"Darcie has a vendetta against me for what happened between us years ago. That's personal. However, when you try and stop my wife and I from performing and making a living, you have gone too far."

Katrina nodded. "I agree, Ciscoe. We cannot make those nightclub owners give you your jobs back. They will have to make that decision for themselves. But if you can show the true connection of the music, then I will take it to the other Civita members for review."

"I will see what I can do," Delia answered, and smiled at Ravi.

***

"Things in life cannot be made straight after becoming crooked," Morrim Goinz began his latest weekly teaching in his office at Kahall Azur. Latisha and I had requested a private meeting with him instead of teaching in the sanctuary with the other parishioners. "Kammbi wants you to appreciate the good as well as the bad, so we as his followers don't get blinded by believing life is supposed to go one way."

Those words came from Book Seven, Chapter Thirteen in the Ryianza section of The Book of Kammbi. The Book of Kammbi was split into two sections: Ryianza (meaning covenant) and Baramesa (meaning promise). The Ryianza section told the story of the early disciples of Kammbi and how their lives were transformed by becoming believers and followers of their God. Those disciples were from the South Country, a land on the other side of the Omarra Sea. The Kammbi religion was created in the South Country several hundred years before it came to this land. The last book of this section contained Kammbi's words of wisdom on how his believers and followers should live.

The Baramesa section told the story of Oscar Ortega, Kammbi's greatest disciple, and his attempt bring the religion to this land. Kammbi requested that Oscar Ortega cross the Omarra Sea to find new believers and followers of the religion. The first six books of the Baramesa section chronicled Oscar's travels in the region, north of the Great Forest, and how he laid the foundation for the religion to take shape in that part of the land. The last book in that section spoke of Oscar's Prophecy told to him by the Eternal Comforter about how all of Kammbia would become believers and followers of Kammbi. Oscar Ortega attempted to follow out that prophecy but failed when he first arrived into the region, south of the Great Forest, near the city of Charlesville. Two hundred fifty years later, Diondray Azur attempted to fulfill the prophecy. Did he succeed? Well, having a morrim and diakonos from the city of Issabella teaching from the Book of Kammbi in our city was an indication that he did.

However, that day's teaching was not from the Baramesa section of the Book of Kammbi. Morrim Goinz went to the last book of the Ryianza section to get Kammbi's words of wisdom. I had read that section several times and those words the morrim said always confused me. I did not understand why a God would not want to straighten what was crooked in life for his believers and followers.

"A life of being a believer and follower in Kammbi does not mean he will remove all the bad things from our lives. Life will become crooked and as believers and followers of Kammbi we must learn how to handle it. And we need to lean on the guidance of the Eternal Comforter, our gift as believers and followers, to get us through the bad things in life," the morrim continued.

I glanced at my wife and saw the disapproval on her face.

"Why should we believe in a God who does not want to take the bad things away in our lives?" Latisha asked. "We might as well believe in ourselves if that's the case."

Morrim Goinz smiled. "Sister Latisha, I'm surprised at your comment. You are usually a close listener. My prior comment stated that we must lean on the guidance of the Eternal Comforter. It is our gift as believers and followers. Kammbi gave us that gift. He will always be with us. But that does not mean he will take away the bad things from our life. Otherwise, people will treat God like some kind of magical charm. Just rub on it when you are in trouble. Kammbi does not work that way. He wants connection with his believers and followers. Real connection comes from the good and bad things in life. Not just the good things."

Latisha pressed the morrim. "I understand that we need to lean on the Eternal Comforter for guidance when the bad things happen. That gift from Kammbi connects us to him as believers and followers. However, the entire Book of Kammbi talks about obedience to him as the blessing. Obey and you will receive your reward. In Book Three of the Ryianza section, the disciple Jorge states it directly. So it seems that as believers and followers of Kammbi, our obedience should make Kammbi remove anything bad that happens to us."

I watched Morrim Goinz nod his head and smile again at Latisha's comment. My wife would ask questions until she got an answer that made sense to her. I had to learn this during our marriage. Latisha had pressed me with her questions on why we should dance a certain way for a performance. She didn't take the first answer from anyone if it did not make sense to her.

"There's the close listener I have come to know," Morrim Goinz replied. "You are correct that Disciple Jorge stated in his book the command from Kammbi, 'Obey and you will be blessed by me for it.' However, I believe you left out that Disciple Jorge had a problem with liquor. Kammbi did not suddenly remove Disciple Jorge's problem. He made his disciple lean on the guidance of the Eternal Comforter to get him through it. Jorge struggled with his liquor problem throughout his early adulthood and even as a disciple. Could Kammbi have taken that problem away? Sure, he could have. Just because you are obedient does not mean that he will take away bad things. Jorge's obedience finally gave him the blessing of getting rid of his problem through the guidance of the Eternal Comforter."

Latisha nodded. "That was a good answer, Morrim Goinz."

"That was a good answer," I interjected. "Thank you for this private teaching, Morrim Goinz. But as I discussed on the phone, we are definitely dealing with some bad things in our lives currently. As we discussed briefly in the last teaching, Latisha and I have lost our jobs in the Roxie and Penelope District. And they are trying to remove us from performing in The Festival of Josette. It seems that Guanamamma music and dancing is being removed from our city. My ex-companion, Darcie Fendlewiesen, has made it her mission to keep us from dancing the way we love and what represents our city."

Morrim Goinz nodded. "Yes, I got that from the last teaching session. I have heard from the other parishioners about this man named Raphael Reynolds stating that Guanamamma music was stolen from the original people that inhabited this city. He is petitioning the Civita to get rid of this music."

"Correct, Morrim Goinz," I replied. "We have to provide proof to the Civita that Walter Fuente did not steal his music from the Nerdann tribe. The Civita has chronicled Walter's arrival here from the city of Terrance until his death. They have the proof that Guanamamma music was not stolen. I don't know what else they would need as proof?"

"Well, Mr. Reynolds has connected with the people with his claim. There must be an underlying belief that Walter Fuente did take his music from the tribe. Did he not create a designated area for the tribe outside of the city as a gift?"

I nodded. "He did. Latisha and I visited the tribe a few days ago. The tribe elders told us the same thing. However, it was not because he stole their music."

"The tribe elders stated he could not have stolen something that was not his in the first place," Latisha added.

"That's why I wanted to go with the teaching from Kammbi's Book of Wisdom," Morrim Goinz replied. "Life gets crooked for all of us. The key is how to navigate it? Our navigation comes from the Eternal Comforter as believers and followers of Kammbi. Lean into that navigation and it will give us the correct guidance at the right time. People tend to want to straighten out what is crooked immediately. However, trying to make straight what is crooked will cause more crookedness. You have to go through the crookedness to become better equipped for the next time when it happens. I believe this attempt to remove your traditional style of music and dancing is a rejection of the past. People believe that being modern or updated means you discard the past. No, you don't. The past is essential to who we are as people. However, we must learn to embrace the present as well. Life will pass you by. Tradition does have a place in current times. But you will have to bring it in a way they can receive it and not lose the essence of that tradition."

I still did not agree with the morrim's teaching after the session. It made sense in my head but I felt differently in my heart. Why believe in a god if he could not take the bad things away from your life? It seemed that the God Kammbi wanted to allow unnecessary pain for his believers and followers. What was the point of that, especially if you were requiring total obedience from them? I had taken to most of the words in The Book of Kammbi since I got it from Darcie all those years ago. However, I did not agree with this section of The Book of Kammbi. Of course, I did not grow up in this city believing in a god. Walter Fuente was the closest thing we had to a god and now we had someone trying to replace him. That was crooked to me and I wanted to do everything I could to make it straight again.

***

"Walter Fuente is a Thief!"

"Guanamamma music is not our music!"

"It must go from The Festival of Josette!"

Those were the words I heard shouted on the steps of the Civita Building in the Fork District near the city's center. Raphael Reynolds led a march from the Wall of Walter's Declaration in the Roxie and Penelope District to the Civita Building. That was a four-mile stretch and he had gathered a significant crowd to join him.

Latisha and I made it to the front of the marching crowd where Raphael stood on the front steps of the Civita building. Darcie stood next to him and he had several members of the Nerdann tribe on those steps too. The police force created a wall between the marchers and the building. Walter's Grove did not have a lot of marches, but I knew the police force was not going to let them get inside the building.

The Civita building was the largest governmental building in the city and resided on East 1st Street in the Fork District. The Fork District had all the city's government and administrative buildings, including the Regnator's Mansion. It was not a district I visited much, other than to pay my property taxes or utilities. However, it was the starting point for the parade portion of The Festival of Josette and symbolically represented the power of Walter's Grove.

The Civita was a five-member council that governed the city. Even though we elected a Regnator every four years to be seen as the city's leader, it was the Civita that truly ran the city. The Regnator was a figurehead position.

All petitions had to be made to the Civita and it was their decision to accept or deny the petition. Raphael Reynolds filed his petition thirty days prior to The Festival of Josette and now with ten days left before the festival, he had decided to put the pressure on the Civita. However, those five members would never be pressured into making a decision due to a march.

"Guanamamma music was stolen from our people," one of the Nerdann tribe members began. I recognized him from the last Raphael speech at the Wall of Walter's Declaration. "Walter Fuente came to this area 170 years ago from the east. He wanted to create a new musical style and he lived amongst my ancestors. Learned our ways. Learned our music. Learned our dancing. What did we get for it? Pushed out of this city and forced into a designated area. He declared it as a gift. What kind of gift was that? A gift from a thief!"

The crowd yelled back that last sentence in unison as the other tribe members began playing the timbau drums.

"Let's show what is the city's real music!" Raphael Reynolds shouted after shouts from the crowd died down. "C'mon Darcie, let's dance."

Darcie had a big smile on her face as she took Raphael's hand. She wore a fitted fire-red dress with silver trim on the sleeves. The nightclub owner wore several thick silver necklaces and bracelets. Darcie was dressed for the occasion.

Raphael pulled her close and started gyrating his hips. Darcie followed his motion as the tribe members played the timbau drums faster. Some in the crowd began to form couples and dance like Raphael and Darcie.

"This is Walter's Grove's real music and dancing. Everybody say Piccanta!" Raphael bellowed.

The crowd followed his command.

Everybody say Piccanta!

Everybody say Piccanta!

Raphael had the crowd in the palm of his hand once again. He knew how to work up a crowd and was a natural leader. It was going to be hard to convince the crowd otherwise.

The Nerdann tribe members slapped the timbau drums harder and created a deeper sound coming from the instrument. Raphael gyrated behind Darcie. She had the biggest grin on her face as she shook her sizeable backside in sync with the drumming. I knew she had wanted to dance like this for a long time. We used to have numerous arguments about how Guanamamma dancing was too formal and rigid. She would counter that the kind of philosophy for Guanamamma dancing was a contradiction to our city's culture. A musician founded this city with his two wives. A city's district was named in their honor and he made a declaration that the city would be built from music, dancing, and love. It did not make sense that Guanamamma dancing would be so formal. Darcie had always believed Walter Fuente did not create Guanamamma dancing but the wealthy of the West Walter's Grove District did instead. They wanted to keep the regular citizens of the city in check by creating a dance that showed the city in a positive light instead of its true nature. However, Piccanta dancing had come along and she believed it truly represented Walter's Grove.

The front part of the crowd had turned into a party with people forming into couples and dancing like Raphael and Darcie. She began dancing with another member of the crowd and continued to gyrate her hips and backside to the pulsating timbau drums. Raphael was not going to pressure the Civita into accepting his petition today. However, he was making an impression with this crowd and the belief that Piccanta music was what the people of Walter's Grove wanted.

Chapter 8

Raphael Reynolds made quite the impression with his march and the Civita had an emergency meeting the next day to decide if they would accept or deny his petition.

Delia told me over the phone after our practice that the Civita would vote on Raphael's petition in two days. There were only eight days left before the Festival of Josette and I did not have any evidence that Walter Fuente did not steal Guanamamma music from the Nerdann tribe. Also, I had learned those Nerdann tribe members that played at the march with Raphael brought their own evidence to the Civita to back up their claim that Walter Fuente stole their music. What evidence did they have? If that evidence was true, then was the chronicling of our city's history at the Civita a lie?

I told Delia I was invited to return to the designated area for the Nerdann tribe. They had more to show me about Walter's connection to them. I was supposed to wait until they summoned me to return. However, time was running out and I needed to see what they had to show me. Delia said she would set up the meeting for the next day. I hoped they accepted her request.

***

We had our latest teaching session in the middle of the Viddhana neighborhood just across from the Hoymala Temple. Ravi asked if Latisha and I could do a teaching session for the neighborhood. It would be the first time a non-Viddhana person would do something like that for the Viddhana people. We were looking forward to the opportunity.

The Hoymala Temple was the center point of the neighborhood where the two main streets Ave Chinnai and Ave Kannada met. Ave Chinnai went north to south through the neighborhood and Ave Kannada went west to east through the neighborhood. Ravi explained the Hoymala temple was built at the meeting point of those two streets in honor of their god, Hoymala. Hoymala always had to be placed at the center point of everyone's lives in the neighborhood. The place of worship for the Viddhana people covered several blocks and was one of the largest buildings in the city.

We were in a park across from the west side of the temple. There was a large paved section surrounded by trees that created an arena-like atmosphere. Ravi said Bismilla and Parvah's enthusiasm about our teaching session got a lot of people from the neighborhood to come. There were at least forty people besides Latisha and myself. Ravi and Bismilla helped us by forming couples and creating space where each couple could dance with enough room. Ravi spoke in the traditional Viddhana language to loosen everyone up. I heard laughter from several couples and they were ready to follow our instruction.

"I want to thank all the attendees here for our first teaching session of Guanamamma dancing with Ciscoe and Latisha Maldonado in the neighborhood," Ravi announced. "As you know, my niece Bismilla and her friend Parvah have attended several teaching sessions with Ciscoe and Latisha in the East Walter's Grove District. Bismilla thought it would be a great idea if they had one of their sessions here in the neighborhood. And I agreed it would be a great opportunity to create a deeper connection amongst each other. I hope you all learn something from today's teaching session."

We stood next to Ravi as the students bowed to us. I returned a bow of my own and Ravi whispered to me that I did not have to do that. The bow given from his people was a gesture of respect towards their visitor and never meant for reciprocity.

"Before we get started, my husband and I would like everyone to face their partner," Latisha said. "We know that Lavanny dancing does not have the man and woman touching each other while dancing together. We respect that custom. But with Guanamamma dancing, the partners must face other and touch. Ravi told us that would be okay for the session. Can we do that?"

The students followed Latisha's instruction. I heard more laughter from several of the couples as they got into position. It was nervous laughter but not uncomfortable. My wife made sure the men had their hands in the correct place on their partners and the women felt comfortable as their counterpart was holding them.

"Our first lesson for Guanamamma dancing is without music," I stated. "A lot of people from the rest of the city's districts believe that Guanamamma dancing is about dancing to the music. It is not. It is about listening to your body and dancing to your natural rhythm and how it connects with your partner. Learning the entire dance without the music gets you attuned to the natural dancing rhythm everyone has."

"Guanamamma dancing begins with being in the correct position," I continued. "I will hold my wife's right hand with my left hand. Then I will place my right hand in the middle of her back. The men lead in Guanamamma dancing and my right hand is the guide hand. Men, don't squeeze your partner's hand or back. As the lead, you are guiding your partner."

I watched the couples followed the instruction. Latisha walked amongst them to see if they were in the proper position. She corrected several of the couples' stances and I could hear the nervous laughter once again. I knew this was not their custom, but I explained how important it was for the men to lead in Guanamamma dancing and how the women must follow. It was a dance based on trust. And that trust created the communication and connection of the dance.

"Guanamamma dancing is about connection with your partner. Make sure you are always looking at each other while dancing. You need to notice the facial expression and body language at all times," Latisha said.

I noticed several of the women amongst the couples would look down or away from their male partner. Ravi explained on the phone last night that Viddhana women did not look at their men while engaging in this kind of activity. I countered his explanation by emphasizing why the women needed to look their partners in the eyes. Their eyes would tell the men leading them if they were dancing correctly and it created the communication between the dance partners. This was what Raphael Reynolds got wrong with Piccanta dancing. Dancing was never just about movement. It was a major component for sure. But the communication and connection between dance partners was just as important as movement.

Ravi understood but told me most of the men objected when he shared with them this aspect of the dance. But the women spoke up and said they would make the adjustment. I thanked Ravi for sharing that aspect of the dance and allowing the students to decide if they were okay with it.

"The main dance step of Guanamamma dancing is the back-and-forth step," Latisha said, as she walked amongst the couples. "This step is primary for all three points of the dance. Men you must learn how to do the step correctly. If you do, then your partner will follow you with ease. If you don't learn this step correctly, your partner will not be in connection with you and will lose trust in your ability to lead in this dance."

I watched the men as Latisha gave that instruction. I could sense that they were not used to getting instruction from a woman. They mostly had blank stares on their faces, but Ravi told me they would cooperate during the teaching session. Learning how to lead with the back-and-forth step is essential to Guanamamma dancing.

"Men, move forward with your left foot," Latisha continued. "Women will step back with the left foot. Then the men will step back with the right foot. Women, move forward with your right foot. Keep your posture straight and men keep your guide hand in the small of your partner's back. Don't squeeze, as my husband mentioned earlier. Just guide your partner."

The men led their partners as they walked through the step. Latisha checked their postures and corrected several couples in the back as a few men stumbled while doing the step. My wife had the students repeat it a few times and about thirty minutes into the session, most of the couples felt comfortable doing it. Ravi spoke in traditional Viddhana language and that helped with any frustration the students had.

My wife and I walked through all three points of the dance after teaching the back-and-forth step. The couples followed and walked through the entire dance as well. I noticed the blank stares from the men begin to evaporate as they noticed the triangular pattern to Guanamamma dancing.

"We danced a similar pattern in traditional Viddhana dancing called Pyreform," Ravi remarked. "It is one of the oldest Viddhana dances that came from our homeland, Kanataka."

Several couples nodded in agreement with his comment and continued going through the entire Guanamamma dance as the

Lavanny musicians started playing music behind us. Ravi had a huge smile on his face and we knew this teaching session was a success. How could Walter Fuente have stolen this music and dancing when another group of people took to it so easily? The Civita needed to see this teaching session and reject Raphael's petition.

***

The Nerdann tribe elders agreed to Delia's request. Latisha and I headed to the designated area the next evening. It was only five days before The Festival of Josette and I was eager to find out the tribe's further connection to Walter Fuente. Hannar brought us back to the center section of the area and I saw the elders of the tribe form a circle. It was the five elders from our previous visit plus three more in the circle. They had formed an alternating pattern of man and woman. The elder closest to us began chanting in the same dialect I heard earlier. His voice was high-pitched and I had to place my hands over my ears. Latisha did the same.

"Please remove your hands from your ears," Hannar asked politely.

Latisha and I obeyed his request and the rest of the elders joined him in the chanting. The high pitch was gone and the chanting sounded musical. The elders began to move in a back-and-forth step like we did in Guanamamma dancing and the closest female elder to us grabbed the timbau drum that was on the ground in front of her. She began playing the instrument as the other elders moved in a circle. Fire erupted from the center of the circle as she played.

The timbau calls us
The timbau creates the rhythm of our people
The timbau speaks through our ancestors
The timbau draws those to it who know how to use it

The timbau honors those who know how to play it
The timbau understands the cycle of life

The fire turned into a sky-blue light and created a thick vapor that drifted above the circle. I placed my arm around Latisha's waist and pulled her close to me. She was transfixed by the vapor but placed her arm around my waist too.

I returned to looking at the vapor and it changed into a face. The female elder stopped playing the timbau. The face looked familiar.

"Ciscoe Maldonado…" the face said softly.

"I'm here."

"There is an accusation from someone in my city who believes that I stole my musical style from the Nerdann tribe."

"This is true," I replied softly. "The accuser believes the music you created is not the city's true music."

The face was Walter Fuente. How could they bring him back from the dead? I'd seen his face on the album covers at my house. And this face looked just like those covers. The silver hair and beard. The large eyes. The mischievous smile. Those features made up his face. How could they create such a thing?

"I'm still dead. The tribe has connected to my spirit because of how I honored their music and instruments," Walter's face continued. "This accuser has promoted a new music to replace what I created, and calls it the true music of Walter's Grove."

I nodded and glanced at Latisha. She was transfixed on his face.

The face drifted away from the circle and floated over us. My fear subsided as he continued talking.

"You both have honored Guanamamma faithfully. The music I helped create along with the Nerdann tribe. It can never be replaced by another musical style that is not from the spirit. The one who speaks falsely about me does not understand the actual history of how

Guanamamma music was created when I arrived from Terrance. I will show you."

Walter's face drifted back inside the circle. The elders returned to their movement in the circle and the female elder played the timbau drum again. The face turned into a large rectangle and the vapor got thick around us. A blue light appeared and then I saw a young Walter Fuente playing the timbau drum with the tribe. One of the tribe members was showing him how to play the instrument. Also, I saw Walter Fuente playing some of his music and the tribe members began playing as well. Then I saw dancing from the tribe to the right of the musicians. It was Guanamamma dancing. They moved in step with the timbau drum, pandretta, and altophone horn. The men led their women partners perfectly. The back-and-forth step, the twirl, and the three points of the entire dance were done. The tribe danced it well. It was just like my father told me as a child. The best dancers of Guanamamma were the tribe members and he wanted to dance to the music just as well as they did. Walter Fuente and the tribe musicians were smiling and playing so well.

The blue light flashed again. This time it was in the city. It looked like the Roxie and Penelope District. Walter Fuente was playing in front of a crowd with members of the Nerdann tribe as the band. People were dancing and it looked like a cross section of the entire city. I was trying to recognize the landmark behind them. Walter moved to the side slightly and I knew that landmark. It was the Wall of Walter's Declaration. He was making his declaration of what the city of Walter's Grove would become.

If a man wants to marry more than one wife, it will be allowed in this city. I will never create (or allow anyone else to create) a law prohibiting anyone from loving as many people as he or she wants. This will be a city built from the spirit of music, dance, and love. Nothing else. I declare it on this day, the eighth of Nayur, year 94 A.O.A.

Also on this day, I want to honor the Nerdann tribe as the co-creator of Guanamamma music. My arrival here in this part of the region South of the Great Forest has created a city for all its citizens. However, we have pushed out the native residents and their way of life. That was not my intention upon my arrival as I was following a vision given to me by the Goddess Marrimba. Good intentions can lead to bad outcomes whether you want them or not. I want to state publicly and for history where my music came from. Without their contributions, the city's music would have not existed. Please let the record show that the Nerdann tribe is just as responsible for Guanamamma music and they will always be recognized for their contribution.

I wanted to create music from every citizen of this city. As you can see, I have Nerdann tribe members in my band as well as someone of the Viddhana people from the southwestern section of Walter's Grove. The Viddhana people took to this music after their arrival in this area from their homeland, Kanataka. And their music has some of the same elements as Guanamamma music. This music represents all of us, not just the one who created it. May the record show that now and forever.

I did not know this part of the history. It was never mentioned in school. My father talked about Walter's Declaration all the time when I was kid. But he never mentioned that Fuente honored the tribe on that same day, or that he had Nerdann tribe members in his band on that day too. He had some of the Viddhana people in the band as well, and they connected to the music shortly after arriving into this area. Both groups were just as much responsible for the creation of the music as Walter. He later stated that the timbau drum and pandretta were the main instruments of this city and any musical style created in Walter's Grove could not exclude them.

The vapor returned and turned back into Walter's face.

"I have never stolen a musical style from anyone, as you just watched. The Nerdann tribe shared their music with me and allowed it to be incorporated with my musical style. The Viddhana people embraced the music too. The one who speaks falsely of me will find out with the rest of the city at the proper time. Ciscoe and Latisha Maldonado, we will be with you because of how you have honored the music. Here's something for you as I depart."

The face dissipated and a glowing blue triangle drifted to me. I reached out to touch it and felt the object enter my body. I saw a blue glowing light everywhere.

***

"You slept for sixteen hours, my love," Latisha said to me as I stood up in our bed.

"Oh no! I missed the Civita's vote on Raphael's petition. I needed to show them what we were shown at the designated area."

Latisha had a forlorn look on her face. "We did miss it. They have voted to accept Raphael's petition. Guanamamma music will be removed from The Festival of Josette going forward."

My wife wrapped her arms around my body and pulled me closer. I was numb.

"I did everything I could to be a part of the festival," I said, after I released myself from Latisha's embrace. "The Civita decided to believe a lie instead of truth!"

I dropped to my knees next to the bed and let the tears flow from my eyes. I did not want my wife to see me crying. The last time I cried was when my mother passed away a few years before. I did not like showing that kind of emotion, even to my wife. I felt it as dropped my head onto our bed. I wanted to show our city that Guanamamma belonged to Walter's Grove, not Piccanta music and dancing.

"Everything will be alright," Latisha said into my ear as I felt her body next to me. "Guanamamma will always have a place in this city."

"How can you say that, my love? The people have rejected it. The Civita believed Raphael Reynolds. They have fallen for the lie!"

Latisha pulled my head from the bed and wiped the tears from my face. "I did not marry the love of my life who loves this music and dancing as much as he does me. All is not lost. Antonio Henderson called after he heard about the Civita's decision to accept Raphael's petition. He wants to meet with us after practice tomorrow."

I placed my hands on my wife's shoulders. She smiled at me and I knew instantly that her last comment was real. "Why does he want to meet with us? He fired us from the Mango."

Latisha ran her fingers through my hair and kissed both of my cheeks. "We will find out tomorrow. You need to eat and listen to some music for the rest of the evening."

I nodded and got up off the floor next to our bed. Latisha grabbed my right hand and I followed her to the kitchen. I had a sense that everything was going to work out, even if I could not see it at that moment.

***

Antonio Henderson pushed his need to clear the air with us to the evening. I got dressed reluctantly and Latisha tried to keep my spirits up with her usual encouragement. My thoughts returned to what happened at the designated area with the tribe and how the blue light entered my body. I remember Diondray telling me when he got something called Boma Essence from the Boma tribe near the city of Adrian. He said it was like his body got plugged into an energy source. I felt the same way. I could feel every sensation in my body like I never had before. It was like being totally connected to your body in a way I could have never thought possible. How long would this blue light stay inside of me?

Latisha and I got dressed for the evening and made our way to the Mango Nightclub. I noticed some red, silver, and green Festival of Josette streamers hanging from the Level Two Clubs' storefront windows. There were streamers hanging from the traffic lights and signposts as we entered the Roxie and Penelope District. The city was starting to get ready for its biggest festival and we were not going to participate in it. I sighed.

"We will dance at the festival, my love," Latisha said as I parked in the Mango Nightclub parking lot. "Once the people see what's inside of you. They will know that Guanamamma music and dancing is the city's real music. I believe what Antonio will discuss with us shortly will help."

"I hope so," I replied, and kissed my wife's left hand before getting out of the car. "I did not want to come tonight. I appreciate Antonio wanting to clear the air. However, I cannot shake the feeling that talking with him will not change what happened when he fired us."

Latisha nodded. "We go back with him for years. And the way he fired us by bringing Brittany and Harrell to dance on the same night we danced did not sit right with me either."

"Yes, my love," I interjected. "That's what I'm feeling. I thought we had a stronger connection with him after all these years. He brought another dannza couple without at least telling us that we were going to be judged by that crowd's reaction to both performances. And we were replaced. That hurt."

"It did, Ciscoe," Latisha stated. "Maybe what that's why he wants to clear the air."

"Yes, you're right. But I have to say something before we head into the club. No matter how this discussion goes, I do not want to dance here at the Mango Nightclub. I want to make sure you are okay with that."

Latisha nodded. "Yes, I'm with you, my love."

I smiled at my wife and kissed her cheek. "I made the right decision sixteen years ago and have never regretted it."

"Same here, Ciscoe Maldonado. You are my favorite bearded, short man in the city."

"Is there another short, bearded man in another city I don't know about?" I said and laughed.

"Fake jealousy will get you lucky at the end of the night," Latisha shot back and smiled.

I continued to laugh as we exited the automobile and headed into the club. It was so important to have the right person in my life. It was one of the best gifts I have ever received.

We did not have to wait in line to get inside the nightclub. The employee stationed at the door led us inside and to the table that Antonio had provided.

"Mr. Jefferson will be with you shortly," the employee said, and returned to his station.

I nodded and looked out at the dance floor. The music player had a Piccanta song playing and people were dancing in the same manner that Brittany and Harrell were from our last time dancing here at the nightclub. Seeing couples dancing like dogs humping each other was not right. Where was the communication? Where was the connection? Where was the harmony between the man and the woman as they moved on the dance floor? Was this the type of dancing the people of the city truly wanted?

"Thank you for accepting my invitation, Ciscoe and Latisha," Antonio said, as he arrived at the table. He kissed my wife on the cheek and then shook my right hand. It did not feel inviting at all.

"First of all, I want to apologize about how everything went down your last night dancing here at the club. I should have told you prior to your performance that Brittany and Harrell were going to be dancers here no matter how well the audience received your dance. I was under a lot of pressure and since the audience was lukewarm for your dance, it was easier to just end our working relationship at that time."

The waiter brought glasses of brownberry juice for everyone at the table. I gulped my juice and replied, "So you were going to fire us no matter what? Why are you telling us now?"

Antonio pulled a cloth and wiped his forehead. He was sweating quite a bit. Was he nervous? Why?

"I don't like being manipulated for a personal vendetta," Antonio answered. "Civita Member Haines Fonseca called earlier that day and said on the phone that I had to get rid of you both as dannzas here in the nightclub. I asked why and Mr. Fonseca said if I wanted to keep my liquor license then I would obey his request."

"He was at our performance at Gancha's!" Latisha remarked.

"I thought he was there to support us," I replied.

Antonio waved the waitress back over and she brought him another drink. It was not brownberry juice. I caught the distinct smell of javann when the glass was placed on the table. "He is a longtime friend of Raphael Reynolds," the nightclub owner added. "Part of Raphael's plan was to make sure that Guanamamma music and dancing be removed from the scene here in the Roxie and Penelope District. The people of West Walter's Grove District can have that music. But the rest of the city needs to have Piccanta music and dancing."

"Mango and The Tajara were the only two nightclubs playing Guanamamma music and allowing us to dance," I replied.

"Correct, Ciscoe. Percy Braxton is my competitor here in the district. However, I found out that Mr. Fonseca gave him the same request as me. So I called Percy to confirm it and found out that Darcie Fendlewiesen was the reason behind Mr. Fonseca's requests. Since Darcie and Raphael are connected, Mr. Fonseca wanted to help out his friend. That's not right. Darcie has an issue with you, Ciscoe. It should have nothing to do with our nightclubs. Percy and I allowed your father to dance at our places and were devoted to the music. You have followed in his footsteps quite well."

I appreciated Antonio's comment about my father. They were friends and my father danced at the Mango for quite some time. I remembered coming with him as a kid and watching how he danced with his partner for that evening's performance. Antonio would get me a glass of brownberry juice and talk about how great a dancer my father was. And I would have big shoes to fill, if I were to become as great a Guanamamma dancer as him. Now, he thought I had filled those shoes.

"We will need evidence to prove that Mr. Fonseca is connected to Raphael and Darcie's plan. The Civita has accepted his petition to remove Guanamamma music and dancing from The Festival of Josette," I said.

Antonio frowned. "I heard this morning. I did not believe the Civita would accept his petition. They have the chronicling of Walter Fuente's arrival here in this part of the region and how he created the music. But I guess some of the Nerdann tribe members' evidence about how Walter forced them into the designated area as a gift is what got the petition accepted."

"Or Haines Fonseca's friendship with Raphael," Latisha said.

Antonio wiped his forehead, reached into his jumpsuit pocket, and pulled out a cassette. "We record all of our conversations here at the club. Here's the recorded conversation of Mr. Fonseca and myself from your last night performing. If this helps to get Guanamamma music and dancing back at The Festival of Josette, then I'm glad to assist in that capacity at least. This is the city's true music."

I reached for the cassette and held it in my left hand. "Thank you, Antonio. Latisha and I appreciate you wanting to talk with us tonight. I will share with you that I did not want to come here tonight. Fortunately, my wife said we should come and hear your explanation. We were hurt by getting fired the way we did. We had a longer relationship with you than any other nightclub owner in this city. Plus, you were a friend of my father and your compliment about how I have filled his shoes was appreciated."

Antonio gave a thin smile. "As I said when we first started this conversation, I don't like being manipulated for someone's personal vendetta. Especially when it involves my nightclub. Mango means everything to me and I'm not going to lose my ability to sell liquor to my patrons when I did nothing wrong. Also, I believe Guanamamma music has represented the city well. And it is a part of our history. We need it at The Festival of Josette, Ciscoe. I want to help in any way I can."

"Thank you again for this cassette," I said. "I'm sorry you got pulled into something I had thought was settled a long time ago."

"Can I ask you something, Ciscoe?" Antonio said.

I nodded.

"Does Darcie blame you for Diondray Azur's dance in our parking lot when he was here in Walter's Grove?"

"Yes, she does," I answered. "You knew about that?"

Antonio nodded. "Diondray talked to me after his dance and

before he left Walter's Grove. The leopards were still in the parking lot after he danced. He told me that he traveled through the entire land of Kammbia due to a prophecy from the book…"

"Book of Kammbi," I interjected.

"Book of Kammbi, correct. And how Darcie did not want him to believe in the prophecy from that book. The religious beliefs are outside of my knowledge. However, he said Darcie blamed you for showing him that you had a copy of that book."

"Darcie and I were companions many years ago when she first came to Walter's Grove," I answered. "She left her birth city of Santa Teresa because of that city's beliefs in The Book of Kammbi. Darcie gave me her copy of that book while we were together. I started reading and have become a believer and follower of its teachings. She has hated me for that ever since. And when I shared the book with Diondray, that fed into her hatred even more."

"She does blame my husband," Latisha added. "She is trying to make him pay because of it."

"I would like to offer our parking lot for you and Latisha to perform," Antonio continued. "It is across the street from the Josette Arena and you can perform at the same time as the Guanamamma Extravaganza."

Latisha smiled at me. There was always a way.

"We will accept your offer," I answered, and shook his hand.

Antonio got up from his seat to attend to some other stuff in the club. We sat and watched couples dance to Piccanta music for a while longer. My first instinct was to leave after our conversation with Antonio. I did not want to watch people dancing to that music. I had seen enough recently to know it was not the same as watching a couple dance Guanamamma.

I looked over at my wife and she was watching a couple to the right of our table dance. The man was about my height with night-colored skin and had a stocky build. His partner stood at the same height and had a neatly trimmed treetop hairstyle that I liked. They were dancing Piccanta style.

"You like how they are dancing?" I asked.

Latisha nodded and looked over at me. "I do. He is not just gyrating behind his partner. They are incorporating Guanamamma steps with their dancing."

I turned to look at the couple and Latisha was right. The man led his partner in several back-and-forth steps and into a twirl before returning to the Piccanta style of dancing.

"His hands are on her hips. The right hand should be in the middle of her back. The left hand clasping her right hand and upright," I said.

Latisha sighed. "My husband. I like where his hands are. She is smiling at him and I can she tell she is good with where his hands are. He can guide her the same way as you do with me."

"Are you serious? The man placing his hands in the incorrect position creates the wrong impression for dancing," I stated.

My wife squeezed my right hand and smiled. "I wish your hands were on my hips as we dance. I would love for you to touch me more like that while we are dancing. I love the smoothness of your hands. It gets me feeling the right way towards you. It would add a little something extra to our dancing."

I was ready to explain how that was not dancing but her comment stopped me in my tracks. "Are you suggesting that we add this element to our dancing? I did not know you felt that way."

"You have been faithful to the tradition of Guanamamma dancing. Gustavoe taught you well and if you don't dance that way it will go against everything that you have learned. However, my love, it does not mean that tradition always has to remain the same. We can incorporate things from the Piccanta style of dance and keep the essence of Guanamamma dancing. Placing your hands on hips is something I would like a lot."

I placed my arm around my wife. "You felt this way for quite awhile?"

"Yes, I have. You are my husband and I know what dancing the correct way means to you. I have followed your lead since we have been married. Maybe it's time to add something to Guanamamma dancing."

I nodded and kissed my wife. What she said made sense. I knew my father would not approve. But he was not here anymore. Maybe I could add something new to our dance.

Chapter 9

I received a package on our front door after our morning practice. It did not have a sender's name or address on it. I had an uneasy feeling about opening the package. When was this package placed on our front door? I could usually hear footsteps when someone came up to the house.

"Let me open it," Latisha said, after I had stared at the package for several minutes.

I handed her the package. She ripped it open and a cassette fell onto the dining room table.

"A cassette?" I said. "From who?"

Latisha pulled out a white letter envelope and opened it.

This conversation between Percy Braxton and Civita Member Haines Fonseca will help you. Mr. Braxton found out that Mr. Fonseca had the same conversation with Antonio Henderson, owner of the Mango Nightclub and gave his version to you. Mr. Braxton wanted to do the same thing and does not like being manipulated, especially over an issue between former lovers. His business, The Tajara Nightclub, should have nothing to do with a vendetta between a competitor in Darcie Fendlewiesen and friends like Ciscoe and

Latisha Maldonado. That should be settled between the direct parties. Also, Mr. Braxton does not like the fact that a Civita member is using The Tajara Liquor License as a part of the vendetta.

Please listen to the five-minute conversation on the cassette and get it to the appropriate party as soon as possible.

I grabbed the cassette from Latisha and put it on the music player. We heard Percy's voice first and I immediately recognized that it was from our last performance at The Tajara. Next, we heard Civita member Haines Fonseca telling Percy that he was to relieve us from dancing at the nightclub and if he wanted to sell liquor at The Tajara he would cooperate. Percy responded in anger and kept asking why he was being involved in something that had nothing to do with him. Haines Fonseca said that someone wanted to make sure that Ciscoe learned a lesson from crossing the wrong person. I knew who that person was.

"I knew I should have given that woman the whipping she needed a long time ago," Latisha erupted. "She has gone too far!"

"A whipping would not change anything, my love. She has been scarred by her past in Santa Teresa. And the way we connected with Diondray Azur reminds her of it. She wants to remove everything from that past," I replied.

Latisha sighed. "I understand that you two had a connection prior to us. But she cannot dictate how you respond to The Book of Kammbi or our connection with Diondray Azur. I know she loves him. Diondray told us that in his last letter from him. She has no right to keep us from dancing at Mango, The Tajara, or The Festival of Josette. And to have a Civita Member help her… she has a serious problem."

"She is stubborn and will do anything to erase her past. Now we have something that will use that stubbornness against her. I will call Delia."

I looked at my wife for several minutes and the anger had not subsided. I had not seen that kind of anger even after our arguments. Latisha usually remained composed under any situation. I would have to spend the rest of the morning calming her down. I knew she wanted to go to Darcie's and give her a whipping. That could not happen. We finally had something to make the crookedness of our lives straight again.

I called Delia and explained that we had two cassettes implicating Civita Member Haines Fonseca's role in blackmailing both nightclub owners. I played her the cassettes and Delia was speechless. She wanted me to bring the cassettes the next morning to the Civita building and she would get me a meeting with Katrina St. Claire. We only had four days left, but this could be the opportunity I needed to get the acceptance of Raphael's petition reversed.

I shared with Delia that Antonio Henderson offered his parking lot as an alternative as we could not perform at The Festival of Josette. He suggested that we dance on the same day as the Guanamamma Extravaganza. Latisha and I had agreed to his offer and planned to spend the next couple of days getting ready for it. Delia liked the idea and wanted the Lavanny musicians and dancers to be a part of the performance. We had planned to include them anyway and were going to the Viddhana neighborhood that afternoon for our teaching session. Delia believed we should focus on the performance instead of trying to get the Civita to change their mind about accepting Raphael Reynolds' position. I agreed reluctantly.

"I know what dancing at The Festival of Josette meant to Gustavoe," Delia said in a soft tone over the phone. "It was his chance to show the city how much he loved the music and dancing. And he has passed that onto you."

"Yes, he has. I still want dance at the festival. We cannot have it replaced by another music that came out of nowhere. My father would have staged his own march at the Civita if he were here."

Delia went silent on the phone for a few seconds. "Correct, Ciscoe. He was a true believer in all aspects of his life. I loved that about him. When he believed in something, he was truly committed to it. I wished I had that same kind of commitment to him."

"Same kind of commitment to him? Where you both together before he met my mother?"

Silence on her end of the phone again.

"Gustavoe and I were companions for a time. I loved your father. We had a passionate companionship. And you were the result of our passion."

"You are my mother? Are you kidding?"

Delia began crying. "You are my son, Ciscoe. My companionship with your father ended shortly before you were born. Gustavoe was determined to make a living as a dannza and perform at the nightclubs in the Roxie and Penelope District. I wanted him to get a regular job and create a stable life for us. But he believed in dancing and would never accept that kind of life. We ended our companionship and I met Manrique a few days later. Manrique had just started his liquor business and I knew he was going to make it in that business. I started our companionship with him and ended up marrying Manrique."

"What about Constance?" I asked.

"Gustavoe started his companionship with Constance after ours ended. I told Manrique that I was pregnant with Gustavoe's child. I thought Manrique would end our companionship right then. This is Walter's Grove and monogamous relationships are a rarity in this city. Manrique said he loved me and wanted to stay together under one condition. I had to create an arrangement with Gustavoe and

Constance to make sure you were taken care of. And you could not know that I was your birth mother. Your father and Constance agreed to the arrangement. Constance could not bear a child of her own and she wanted to be a mother. So we agreed to the arrangement and I thought that it would be the best thing at that time. I was so wrong. I'm sorry, Ciscoe."

I went numb and hung up the phone. Latisha wrapped her arms around me and I felt the tears fall from my face.

I was in a fog for the rest of the day. I did not want to eat or listen to music. Latisha and I did our teaching session in the Viddhana neighborhood and worked with the Lavanny musicians afterwards. But they could tell my mind was somewhere else. I kept seeing visions of Delia and my father together. I sensed the blue light was causing these visions. I knew her story about being my mother was true. Why would she agree to that kind of arrangement? I had called Delia my aunt for many years during my childhood. She was my mother all along? And the woman I called my mother, Constance, was not? Constance died a few years before my father but she raised me as her own. We got along quite well and I missed her. But why would she agree to the arrangement? The desire to be a mother was that strong? As a man, I would never understand that type of connection. I was even more grateful for her now. I wished she were here so I could express it to her. Delia Marie Villanueva was my mother and I was not sure if I could accept it.

***

That evening, Latisha and I had dinner at Saahib's before going to Club Hancock to watch Zakiyah perform again. My wife did not want me walking around the house in a fog after Delia's admission. Delia called several times throughout the day but I did not want to speak to her. Why would a mother give up her child so easily? For love? To help Manrique Villanueva become the biggest liquor business in the city? I could not wrap my head around why Delia would agree to his condition. She loved my father and it was true that being a dannza meant everything to him. Couldn't she have joined him? And found a way to make it work? Latisha accepted I was going to become a dannza and follow in my father's footsteps. Sixteen years later, we found a way to make it work. There were some lean years in the beginning our marriage. Latisha only had one condition: that we were monogamous. As long as I kept our marriage on that level, she would be there. Delia could have done the same thing.

A waitress brought Latisha and I our regular dishes as Saahib sat down with us.

"You saw Walter Fuente's face amongst the tribe," Saahib remarked after I explained our visit with the Nerdann tribe. "How could they bring him back from the dead? "

"Walter Fuente is still dead, brother," Latisha added. "He is connected to the tribe through his spirit. He honored their music and recognized them as co-creators of Guanamamma music. We just saw an essence of his spirit out there."

"Most people of this city know that Walter Fuente honored the tribe in his music," Saahib said. "They have willfully decided to ignore that part of our history."

"Raphael Reynolds has most of the city believing that Walter Fuente stole his music from the Nerdann tribe. And his petition to remove Guanamamma music and dancing from The Festival of Josette was accepted by the Civita," I replied.

Saahib nodded as I finally started eating my tortas. "I heard about that, brother-in-law. I can't believe the Civita accepted his petition. They have the history in their archives. What evidence did Raphael Reynolds provide to show that the archives are incorrect?"

Latisha and I stared at each other for a moment. "Some members of the Nerdann tribe believe Walter's gift of the designated area for them was moved out of the city," my wife said.

"We all grew up knowing that Walter's gift to the tribe was an attempt to keep their way of life together," Saahib said. "Sister, is there something else going on?"

Saahib picked up Latisha's tone of voice. We did not want to mention the cassettes we had received from Antonio and Percy. That information could only be shared with Katrina St. Claire before it went public.

"There is a lot going on, Saahib," she replied. "You and the rest of the city will find out soon."

Saahib glanced at both of us and knew not to ask any more questions. "Well, the truth will always set you free."

I nodded and finished eating dinner. I was glad to have this conversation with Saahib, and Latisha helped ease my mind somewhat about Delia. I needed to find out more about why she would agree to that arrangement before I could truly accept her as my mother.

***

Latisha and I met with Civita member Katrina St. Claire the next morning. We skipped our practice for that meeting. The last time we did not practice in the morning was when my father died. However, Katrina agreed to meet as soon as she got into her office. Delia told her about the cassettes and she wanted to hear them as soon as she could.

Her assistant, Nadine, brought us to Katrina St. Claire's office. Nadine led us through several hallways on the second floor of the Civita building until we reached the offices of all five Civita members. Ms. St. Claire's office was the last one on the right.

"Welcome, Ciscoe and Latisha," Katrina said, as we entered her office.

She had dark brown skin and a wide smile that put me at ease immediately. Katrina's braided hair extended past her shoulders and she dressed in a yellow jumpsuit with a red broach pinned near the pocket area. Katrina's presence felt similar to Latisha's.

"I appreciate you meeting with us, Ms. St. Claire."

"Katrina is good. Ms. St. Claire is my mother."

I nodded and handed her both cassettes. "Got it, Katrina. Here are the cassettes we received from nightclub owners Antonio Henderson and Percy Braxton. My wife and I were surprised that both of them recorded their phone conversations. But they both explained it was a regular occurrence due to the business they were in and if something happened to either one of them there would be something to show what happened."

Katrina opened the envelope and took out the cassettes. She put the cassette that had Wallace's conversation with Civita Member Haines Fonseca on her sound system first. "Oh no! That is his voice," she said and placed a hand over her mouth. "He told me the night we saw your performance at Gancha's that he believed the archives we have about Walter Fuente's arrival here to create our city were accurate. And now he's saying that he believes Raphael Reynolds' claim is the correct history."

"But you accepted his petition," I replied.

"I was the only one that voted against the petition," Katrina continued, and played the cassette that had Percy's conversation. "The other members believed those Nerdann tribe members' story that Walter's gift was his way of moving them out of the city. He had got the foundation of his new music from them and since they would not assimilate into becoming citizens of the city, they had to be moved out."

"We visited with the elders and they stated that Walter Fuente did not steal their music. They freely shared with him. Did any of the Civita members check with the tribe elders?" Latisha asked.

"No, we did not. Haines Fonseca assured us the tribe members that came to the hearing for the petition represented the entire tribe."

I raised my hands in front of my face and saw the blue light glowing just above them. I felt that light race through my body. I could hear Walter's voice in my head. I stood up and fell back on the floor. I heard my wife yelling my name. All I saw was blue light for the next several minutes.

"Ciscoe!"

My wife was behind me and had raised my shoulders up while Nadine sat next to me with a glass of water. I could tell she had given me some of it to drink. The front part of my shirt was wet.

"I saw everything," Katrina said with a pained expression on her face. "The tribe shared their music with Walter freely and they wanted to have the designated area. And we voted to get rid of our city's real music from The Festival of Josette. I'm sorry."

I just realized the blue light had shown Katrina what we witnessed at the designated area with the tribe. I didn't know if they could reverse their decision on the petition. But at least she knew the real history of our music and dancing and why it should have never been removed from The Festival of Josette.

Chapter 10

"The provision of the Eternal Comforter is peace, understanding, trusting in the one who provides, and joy for being alive," Morrim Goinz stated in his latest teaching session at the Kahall Azur.

The Festival of Josette began the next day and I still had a lot to work through with Delia. She had called regularly for the past two days and I refused to talk to her. Latisha tried to get me to understand that the silent treatment would not work in the long term. However, I was not ready to talk to my birth mother. I visited my father and Constance's gravesite that morning before practice and shared everything that had happened in the last thirty days of my life. I wished they were both here because I needed them. But I wondered if Delia would have ever told the truth about being my birth mother if my parents were alive?

"I want to focus on the word *understanding* for today's session," Morrim Goinz continued. "Understanding is a word that we use a lot in my birth city, Issabella. It is spoken of regularly in terms like we must have an understanding of a particular topic. I'm always leery when a word like this one is used too much. It begins to take away from the actual meaning. Words have power and that power can be diluted when it is spoken way too much."

"Doesn't understanding mean the ability to comprehend? Or

having insight?" I replied. Latisha and I sat in our usual spot in the Kahall. There were about thirty parishioners at the Kahall with us.

Morrim Goinz smiled. "You are correct, Brother Ciscoe. Having insight are the main words in your answer. Insight is a key quality in any type of human connection. It seems when people come from different places or have different beliefs that insight into another's perspective can create understanding. Insight like that is in short supply these days."

"Are we capable of having insight?" Latisha asked.

"We are, Sister Latisha. But we must get out of our own way. That's a hard thing to do without having something guiding you from a larger perspective than your own."

"The belief in Kammbi is that larger perspective," I added.

Morrim Goinz laughed gently. "Of course it is, from my perspective, Brother Ciscoe. Why would I be here in this city? Why would I teach in a place that does not have the same belief system? Why would I try to explain that the teachings in The Book of Kammbi can benefit all of us? Understanding can lead to real connection. As believers and followers of Kammbi, we must be understanding towards others that don't share our belief in the one who guides us."

Morrim Goinz closed the teaching session as everyone in the Kahall stood for dismissal. It was interesting how a teaching session could bring up exactly what we were going through. For him to teach on what understanding truly meant could have a greater effect on the city in the days to come. Understanding would not have led Darcie to do everything she could to keep Latisha and I from dancing at The Festival of Josette. Understanding would have made Raphael Reynolds and those Nerdann tribe members appreciate our city's history. Understanding would not have caused Delia to create an arrangement for another woman to pretend she was my actual birth mother. Understanding would be needed if I were going to accept Delia as she claimed. Understanding would be needed more than ever.

***

"Katrina St. Claire presented the cassette tapes to the other Civita members today," Delia said over the phone. She called an hour after we got back from our final practice with the Lavanny musicians and dancers. I placed the phone call on the speaker so Latisha could hear it. "The other Civita members were shocked at hearing Haines Fonseca's voice on the cassette."

"Are they going to play the cassettes for the Regnator?" Latisha asked.

Delia sighed. "Not yet. The Civita Members were divided on bringing that kind of information to the Regnator. Haines Fonseca did acknowledge that was his voice on those cassette tapes. But he will tell the Regnator that he was recorded without his knowledge. And he can use that point in his favor with the Regnator."

"So are they going to let him get away with blackmail?" I shot back. Those were the first words I had said to my birth mother in the past few days.

"They won't, Ciscoe," Delia replied. "This is politics and Katrina has to be in the most advantageous position to bring a charge like that against another Civita Member."

"His voice is on those cassette tapes! What more does she need?"

"My love, Delia is correct. We have to let Katrina handle this correctly. I don't like the politics of it any more than you do. But accusing a Civita Member of blackmail is not so easy, despite the evidence we have presented," Latisha added.

I looked at my wife as she sat next to me. She was taking Delia's side on this one? Latisha placed her hand on my left thigh and began patting it. I could not stay mad with her for long. She knew it. "We should not have to tip toe around with Haines Fonseca. He committed blackmail and that evidence should be used to reverse their decision to accept Raphael's petition!"

"Gustavoe taught you well," Delia started. "The Festival of Josette was just as important as dancing in the Roxie and Penelope District. He wanted to make sure that he danced at our biggest festival every year. And he has made sure you feel the same way. I remember him saying after the first cry when you were born that you were his clone."

I was silent. Latisha had nuzzled against me and kissed my right cheek. Her body was still warm from our lovemaking prior to Delia's phone call. I felt the blue light racing through my body.

I sighed. "Why did you agree to that arrangement with Constance and my father?"

Delia went silent momentarily. "Constance was a good woman and wanted to have children. She had that maternal instinct and your father wanted to have another child with her. But she could not and saw the arrangement as her only chance to become a mother. Your father loved Constance despite their differences. She was not a dancer but accepted that would be the number one thing in his life. Gustavoe knew Constance would take care of you like she had given birth to you. He stayed in a relationship with her for that reason. He wanted to make sure you had stability in your life. I made sure that you never had to worry about anything financially. I almost ended my marriage to Manrique as you started to get older because he wanted to end financial support. That was never going to happen. I made a selfish decision and the least I could do was to make sure you never wanted for anything."

"I called you Aunt Delia as a child," I said softly. "Why tell me now?"

Delia sighed as I heard her choke back tears on the other end of the phone. "Truth hurts but also heals. There were so many times over the years I wanted to tell you, but felt ashamed of my decision to let Constance raise you. I finally had to face up to my selfish decision and tell you."

I did not know what to feel at that moment. Should I be angry? Should I be happy? Delia had made sure I had everything I ever needed growing up. My father would tell me that Aunt Delia had gotten these new clothes for me. Or got me this item for my birthday and so on. I would spend time at her house when Manrique was alive. She had always been a part of my life. I found out from Antonio Henderson that she vouched for me to dance at the Mango. I thought my father helped me with that. Antonio explained that Delia believed I could be just as good as my father. Did she do all these things for me just because of the arrangement?

"You have every right to be angry with me, Ciscoe. But I wanted to tell you the truth and let you know that I love you."

"I love you too, mother," I said, and ended the call.

***

The morning of The Festival of Josette, the front page of our newspaper, *Walter's Grove Ledger,* had the story of Antonio Henderson and Percy Braxton being blackmailed by Civita Member Haines Fonseca. I found out Katrina St. Claire provided the newspaper with the cassettes and the details of those conversations in the story. Our phone rang all morning and we had to turn off the ringer to practice.

Delia came to our home later in the day. I could not stop thinking about her admission as my mother. As much as I wanted to be angry with her for that arrangement, I kept hearing the Morrim Goinz's words from his last teaching session in my mind. Understanding would be needed if we were going to connect as mother and son.

"I still can't believe a Civita Member would stoop this low to blackmail two nightclub owners," Delia stated, as she sat across from us in the living room. "What did he have to gain by getting himself in a situation like this?"

"It is always easier to believe a lie than truth," I said. "Raphael has done a great job in convincing most of the city about Piccanta music. And Haines Fonseca is his long time friend."

My mother nodded and rose from the couch. She walked over to me and extended her arms. I rose from the couch and embraced her.

"I'm sorry, my son. I thought I would not be a good mother for you. And knowing that Constance wanted to be a mother made me accept that arrangement. I wanted to help my husband build the biggest liquor business in the city. We achieved that and it did not take away the decision I had made with you. I'm so sorry."

My mother was sobbing on my shoulder. I was trying to think of the right words to say. "As you said earlier, the truth hurts and heals. Let's start there, mother."

She released me from our embrace and placed her hands on my face. "We can start there, son."

Latisha joined in and embraced both of us. Our family was whole and nothing would break it apart ever again.

"Haines could sidestep one claim of blackmail, but not two of them. And now the newspaper has the story," Delia said after our embrace and returned to her seat on the sofa. "I talked to Katrina before I came here. She was going to implore the members to take the accusations to the Regnator."

"Can the Regnator remove a Civita member?" I asked.

"Even though the Regnator is the symbolic leader in our city's government, he can vote to remove a Civita member from their position," my mother continued. "But that's unlikely, my son. Haines has a good relationship with the Regnator. And the Regnator will not vote to remove him."

"Nothing happens to him?" I replied.

"He will get ridiculed publicly and lose his ability to receive the pension for his time as a Civita member. Also, he will agree to reverse their decision to accept Raphael's petition and beginning next year, Guanamamma music and dancing will return to The Festival of Josette."

"He will stay on as Civita Member."

"Yes."

I sighed. Even though we finally had the upper hand, I didn't like that we had to make a compromise to get it. Wrong was wrong. Haines Fonseca needed to be removed from his position.

"Don't think like your father," Delia said. "Everything in life does not always come out black and white. There is always a shade of grey. And to get something you want, you have to give up something."

"I don't like that. Haines Fonseca needs to be removed from the Civita. Blackmailing regular citizens of this city is wrong. Power cannot be used like that."

"I agree with you," my mother replied. "But his career as a Civita Member will never be the same. His reputation has been ruined and he will be voted out when the next election comes. We will have to accept this as punishment for his actions."

***

The first five days of The Festival of Josette had various events around the city. Every district in the city had a celebration of some kind to acknowledge how Walter Leonardo Fuente founded the city. Replicas of the Wall of Walter's Declaration were on every street corner and food stands were in the center of each district. All the nightclubs in the Roxie and Penelope District opened at sunrise for the entire time of the festival. People went from one district to another district to see which one had the biggest celebrations.

The last day culminated in the Guanamamma Extravaganza. It began with the morning procession in the Fork District called the March of Walter. March of Walter reenacted Walter Fuente's journey from his birth city of Terrance to our part of the region, South of the Great Forest. The Regnator gave a brief oral history of how our city was founded by the musician. March of Walter started on West 1st Street and continued until it met Ave Roxie. Then, the march turned left and continued west until East 1st Street. The march turned right onto East 1st Street and travelled north where it rejoined West 1st Street. Raphael Reynolds tried to get this part of The Festival of Josette removed when his petition got accepted. But the Civita members refused that part of the petition and let him know firmly this part of our city's history could never be removed from The Festival of Josette.

Latisha and I attended the March of Walter procession briefly before we had to get to the Mango Nightclub parking lot to get ready for our performance. Even though it did not get removed because of Raphael's petition, I wanted to make sure I heard the Regnator's reading of the oral history of how our city was founded. However, I was surprised to see Civita Member Haines Fonseca read the city's oral history instead of the Regnator. He had the look of a defeated man as he read the history to everyone. The Regnator and the other Civita members stood next to him with faint smiles on their faces. The crowd booed Haines Fonseca as he read and I realized that my mother was right. He was going to get punished far worse than just being removed from his position as a Civita member.

After the March of Walter procession was The Festival of Josette parade at the marperia. The marperia was just south of the Fork District and north of the Roxie and Penelope District. It was the best people watching area in Walter's Grove. Each district in the city would have various residents create floats reflecting our history. The Civita members would judge which district had the best float and the winning float got the silver key to the city for the year. The people filled the marperia and watch the floats pass by.

However for this year, the parade was removed because of Raphael's petitions and renamed the Piccanta Pageant. The pageant would showcase Piccanta music and dancing while Raphael Reynolds would declare it as the city's true music. Delia explained over the phone last night how Raphael wanted to make sure he got the Piccanta Pageant in the festival to offset the March of Walter. I was glad that I was not there to see that falsehood shared with our people. However, I believed that our citizens would not so easily accept Raphael's version of our city's history and knowing the Piccanta Pageant would only be for this year's festival made me feel at ease. He could have his moment in the sun but the truth of our city's history could never be so easily removed.

Latisha and I were dressed in our customary black and silver dannza outfits. We were standing behind the makeshift stage in the Mango nightclub parking lot. Across the street at the Josette Arena, people were waiting to enter it once the Piccanta Pageant ended. Instead of the Guanamamma Extravaganza that was usually held in the Josette Arena on the last day of the festival, Raphael Reynolds was going to have a huge concert with the best Piccanta musicians in the city. The concert would declare Piccanta music's rightful place in our city's history and culture. I hoped our performance would draw enough people to the nightclub's parking lot to see the music and dancing that actually helped create Walter's Grove.

The Lavanny dancers were dressed in their traditional orange costumes with silver accessories. There were six dancers: three men and three women. Latisha spent the last hour with them going over the routine. She was much better than me at going over the same steps repeatedly. I did not have that kind of patience. I had to get myself ready for our performance and clear my mind of all other thoughts besides the dancing. However, I thought about my father and his teachings about staying in the moment. The man must always lead his partner with tight, crisp steps. Then my thoughts turned to my mother. We had talked more about her relationship with my father. She shared how she met him dancing in the Roxie and Penelope District and how he proposed marriage the second night after meeting her. She rejected his proposal and they were companions for about a year. My mother loved dancing with my father, but he did not have any other ambition or interests. She wanted to be in a relationship with someone who had a future. My mother thought at that time being a dancer was not stable as a career or ambitious enough for her. I realized I was the same way. My life had been about Guanamamma music and dancing. Nothing else besides Latisha interested me. I wondered if I had created a life too narrow for Latisha. She had never mentioned that as a negative in our life together. But after hearing my mother's comment about my father and that I was his clone, I wondered if I had I repeated the same pattern with my wife.

I followed Latisha to a section behind the stage where I could see the Lavanny dancers and musicians perform. I was looking forward to seeing them perform traditional Viddhana music for the entire city.

"What are you doing here? "Latisha said.

I turned and saw Darcie standing across from us. She looked crestfallen. I had no idea why she was here.

"You have caused enough damage," my wife continued. "You should not have come here. We have nothing to say to you."

Darcie's eyes watered. "I would like to talk to Ciscoe for just a moment," she said in a soft voice that I had never heard from her before.

"We are getting ready to perform. You had your chance to speak about what you tried to do for a long time. You should leave."

"Please Latisha. I would like to speak to Ciscoe."

I placed my hand on Latisha's right shoulder. My wife turned towards me and I nodded.

"We have a couple of minutes before we perform," I replied. "But you have to say it to both of us."

My wife nodded and Darcie sighed.

"Okay. I wanted to apologize for my actions," Darcie started. "I let my hatred of my upbringing in Santa Teresa guide how I acted. I hate The Book of Kammbi and what it represents. I did give you that book as a gift and blamed you for showing Diondray that you had it. I loved him and wanted him to stay here in Walter's Grove. I knew he was going to leave and try to fulfill that stupid prophecy. I blamed you for that, Ciscoe, and I was determined to get revenge. The only way to get revenge was to take away the one thing you love the most besides Latisha. I apologize."

Darcie's comment seemed genuine and I had to give her credit for coming to apologize. But I had no comforting words for her.

"Thank you for your apology," I replied. "I wanted to show Diondray that we had a copy of The Book of Kammbi to let him know there were people south of the Great Forest who honor its teachings. He was going to do his part in attempting to fulfill Oscar's Prophecy. You should have known that. "

"Those teachings are backwards, Ciscoe. They want all women to be married and pregnant by the age of twenty-one. Only men get to be whatever they want and have it blessed by that God, Kammbi."

"What about Teresa? Or Alicia? Both of those women appear prominently in The Book of Kammbi."

Darcie straightened up and she seemed to get her spirit back. "Those are exceptions to the rule. Yes, I know my birth city Santa

Teresa is named after one of the women in The Book of Kammbi and she was considered a great woman of that religion. But the people of my birth city have used that rule to create the concept that the only option for a woman is to be a man's wife and mother to his children."

"There is nothing wrong with being a wife and mother," Latisha added.

"I agree with that, Latisha. Especially in this city where marriage is a rarity, but it should be done on an equal footing—not just about what the man wants."

"This is not the time to argue about the teachings from The Book of Kammbi. You wanted to take away something that means the most to me outside my marriage to Latisha. Your actions went too far and I thank you for coming here to apologize. I believe you should leave now."

I found out from Delia that the Civita took away her liquor license for a year as punishment in her role with Haines Fonseca. She protested their decision but had to accept it or lose her nightclub, Darcie's for good. Darcie had no chance but to accept the Civita's punishment for what she had done. I watched her wipe the tears from her eyes and leave.

***

Viddhana!

I heard that word bellow throughout the entire parking lot as the Lavanny dancers and musicians went onto the stage. I looked around and saw some people leaving the line to get into the arena to come see us. I took some deep breaths and clasped my wife's hand. She smiled and I felt reassured.

The first Lavanny musician began playing the altophone horn in a low muted sound. She covered the horn with her hand to get that sound. The three women dancers started moving from left to right in front of the horn player. The musician kept playing the same sound as the dancers began their first step with the left foot forward and alternated with the right foot. They did those steps several times as the women grabbed the loose fabric from their pant legs and waved it like a flag. The Lavanny dancers had big smiles and I could tell they were enjoying this opportunity to perform.

A second musician began playing the timbau drum. The timbau drum was strapped to his chest instead being held between the legs. The musician hit the instrument lightly and the drum sound synchronized with the horn sound. The female dancers rose off their right feet and twirled in place. They were still waving the loose fabric from their pant legs.

"They are moving beautifully," Latisha said softly.

I nodded and kissed her on the cheek.

A third musician started playing the guitar and synchronized his sound with the other musicians. Then the three male Lavanny dancers joined their female partners and began moving in the same formation. The crowd had gotten bigger and erupted with applause.

I placed my arm around Latisha and squeezed her close to me. "They love it."

"I knew they would. People of this city love a performance."

"That's true," I replied, while the crowd's applause started to fade.

The altophone horn player changed her sound to a long wail as the other musicians stopped playing. The Lavanny dancers faced each other and moved in a circle to the horn solo. The male dancers reached out their left hands to their female partners. The female dancers moved closer to their partners and grabbed their hands. The horn player finished the solo with another long wail as the other musicians joined in. The dancers interlocked their fingers and moved left to right. Ravi had explained to me during one of the practices this introductory dance was called the nimmi or the invitation. The Lavanny dancers began each performance with a nimmi. It signified to the audience their invitation to the dance. The nimmi was the first section of the three-part traditional Viddhana dance. The other two sections: maddhi or "the middle" and sammi or "closing" completed the dance. Latisha and I were going to dance after the sammi section.

The guitar player started the maddhi section of the dance. He played fast as the dancers formed a single-file line and did a twirl in sync with the music. Seeing the orange and silver from the dancers' clothes was beautiful. The altophone horn played a soft, whisper-like sound as the dancers broke away from the single-file line and continued twirling in their own section of the stage. I glanced at Latisha and noticed that she was totally absorbed in the performance.

The timbau drum player joined in with the guitarist. The dancers returned to face each other and moved in a back-and-forth Guanamamma step with the men leading. The timbau drum sound was heavy and rhythmic. My left foot tapped the ground and I was ready to dance. The male Lavanny dancers grabbed hold of their partners and began leading each one into a side-step movement. They were incorporating Guanamamma dance steps into this section of their traditional Viddhana dance. Latisha faced me and we kissed. I could feel her excitement, as I knew she practiced this part of the dance with them a lot over the last few days. The Lavanny dancers executed it perfectly.

The Lavanny musicians ended the music as the dancers exited the stage to the right. I took a deep breath and Latisha grabbed my right hand. There was a moment of silence as the musicians finished with their music.

Viddhana!

The timbau player ended his portion with their rallying cry. The crowd erupted with applause. I knew they would nail their performance. The city needed to see the Viddhana people share some of their heritage at The Festival of Josette. The stage lights came on. Zakiyah and the band were on the right side of the stage. The band started playing a Guanamamma song.

Why do people believe in a lie?
Than the truth
That has been with us all the time
Every person knows
What is wrong
And what is right
We are all connected
In this city
And there was a man
Who saw the vision
And acted on it
The truth of it that
Will set us free…

Zakiyah sang that first verse so elegantly that I almost got lost in the song. Latisha tugged on my shirt to snap me out of that musical trance. I led Latisha with the back-and-forth step three times during the first verse. I sang that verse under my breath as we danced. *The Truth Will Set Us Free* by Natalia Havana was Constance's favorite song. She played it in the house all the time during my childhood. Constance would sing the lyrics every time my father left the house to go dance at the nightclubs in the Roxie and Penelope District. Even though she did not give birth to me, I appreciated her raising me as her own and being in my life. I wished she were here to see us dance to her favorite song.

Why do we push away the past
And where we came from
For the sake of wanting something new?
Don't we know
Without what happened before us
Or the one who laid the path
There can never be real progress
The past is not something
To be burdened with
Or carry around like dead weight
It is a reminder
That the truth
Will set us free

I twirled Latisha three times after we reached the second point of the dance. I loved the way her dress flared out at the bottom while twirling. It made her look magnificent.

Why don't we embrace
What really happened before us
To accept the history and tradition
Doesn't have to live in a book
Or be recited from memory
But it is a living and active part
Of who we are
And citizens of this great city
Must share it from generations
To come
So that truth
Will set us free

I pulled Latisha towards me and placed my hands on her hips as we reached the third point of the dance. She began moving her hips to the rhythm of the song. My wife grinned. She knew this was a big step for me to add this part to our dance. We moved back and forth with our bodies close together during the rest of it. The crowd erupted in applause as the music faded. I kissed my wife and wrapped my arms around her.

We continued to dance as the band moved the song into Piccanta music. I did not expect that from Zakiyah and the band. But when she started dancing, the crowd followed her. Latisha and I added some of those dance steps during the last couple of practices. I was not ready to become a Piccanta dancer but holding my wife close felt right. The crowd cheered as we danced. The crooked had not only become straight. It had created a new line.

I looked at the crowd and saw people packed together. I could feel the energy of the crowd and the blue light started racing through my body. I knew I had to brace before I only saw a vision of blue.

My Love…

I knew that was Latisha calling me and then I heard these words.

I've heard there is a new style of music that has been created recently. It has come to replace what I created when I first arrived here 170 years ago.

There is an accusation from a musician that I stole my musical style from the native people of this area. People of this city should want the truth. People of this city should demand the truth. People of this city will get the truth.

I could feel Walter Fuente's voice throughout my entire body while I could only see blue light. His voice faded and I heard music. Music that was familiar. Music that my parents played during childhood. I knew Walter was showing everyone in the parking lot how he created Guanamamma music.

After receiving the vision from the Goddess Marrimba, I knew I had to leave my birth city of Terrance. When I arrived here, the Nerdann tribe was the first greet to me, my wives, and our small group of fifty. I heard the sound of the timbau drum and knew I must have it in my music. I played for the tribe for seven days straight and asked them if I could incorporate the timbau drum into my music.

Walter's voice faded again and I heard a new voice throughout my entire body.

The tribe elders have listened to your music for the past seven days, Walter Fuente. We have elected to share our music with your music to create something new. The cycle of life has told us it's time for something new to be brought here. This new music will stand the test of time because of how you asked us instead of taking from us. And you honor our ways by playing for us as we asked you to. We will share our music gladly.

"Walter Fuente did not steal his music from the Nerdann tribe!" a voice from the crowd said.

The blue light swirled in my vision and I knew what people were going to see next. I could feel my body go limp and absorb the energy from the blue light until everything went black.

"My love, you're back!" Latisha said as she held me in her arms.

Delia, Zakiyah, and Ravi were all standing over me. All of them had looks of amazement on their faces.

"My son, I did not know you were that connected to the Nerdann tribe," my mother said softly. "People saw Walter give his declaration and he said the tribe were co-creators of Guanamamma music. I did not know that part of his declaration."

"We were not taught of his declaration in school. I always grew up believing that Walter was the sole creator of Guanamamma music," Zakiyah added.

"Walter Fuente had a member of my people in his band and they were at his declaration," Ravi remarked. "Viddhana people have been a part of this city since the beginning. Walter Fuente accepted my people when we arrived in this city. I never knew this part of our history."

I nodded. "I did not know about this part of the history until our visit at the designated area for the tribe. Latisha and I saw the same thing everybody here just witnessed. I don't know why this was omitted from our history. But the truth will set you free."

Author's Note

I had planned to write the fourth and final novel of the Diondray's Chronicles series after I completed Diondray's Roundabout. Diondray's Roundabout was book three and the novel I most enjoyed writing at that time. However, there were two secondary characters from that novel, Ciscoe and Latisha Maldonado that demanded their own story.

As a storyteller, I've learned to trust your storytelling instincts and tell a story that you did not expect too. Ciscoe and Latisha Maldonado deserved their own novel and Ciscoe's Dance was the result of their demands.

I love books about the arts (books, music, art, and dancing) and how culture interacts with those aspects of life. The novels of Brazilian author Jorge Amado and Canadian author Charles de Lint come to mind with their tales of the arts and culture. Their books have given me inspiration to write the kinds of stories I want for my fictional world of Kammbia.

Ciscoe's Dance represents the kinds of stories I want to tell for the rest of my writing career. This story deals with cultural appropriation, past versus present, and how music and dance can bring people from various backgrounds together. These types of stories continue to peak my interest and I want to engage my readers with going forward.

I hope my readers enjoyed this story on a basic storytelling level as well as the elements between the lines. What astounds me is how family comes to the surface especially in the relationship between Ciscoe and Delia Villanueva. My early readers comment on their relationship and how Delia's revelation surprises them.

Ciscoe's Dance took longer than I expected to complete. But, I realize this novel is a watershed mark for me personally and professionally. If this story can allow you to escape from your everyday life for a few hours or days, then I have done my job as a storyteller. Thank you for reading.

Thanks for reading **Ciscoe's Dance** and joining on another adventure in the world of Kammbia.

Ciscoe's Dance is the first book in a duology called the Dance and Listen Series. The second book, Cassandra's Revelation will be released in the fall of 2022. However, each book in this series can be read as a standalone story.

Also, I have my Diondray's Chronicles Series that you can read if you want to know more about the world of Kammbia.

Diondray's Discovery, Diondray's Chronicles Book 1

Diondray's Journey, Diondray's Chronicles Book 2

Diondray's Roundabout, Diondray's Chronicles Book 3

If you are an avid reader, you can check out my Marion's 25 Book Review series. I have been a book review blogger since 2011 and have reviewed over 200 books on my blog, marion-hill.com. I have created a book series featuring 25 books I have reviewed that I consider as favorites. I believe in reading widely from genre to literary fiction to non-fiction. Reading is the easiest way to travel to new worlds and feed your curiosity!

Marion's 25 Volume 1

Marion's 25 Volume 2

I will be releasing Marion's 25 Volume 3 in 2022. Stay tuned!

You can connect with me on my blog:
marion-hill.com

or on Instagram:
@marhill31

A Note from Marion…

If you've enjoyed this book, I would be grateful if you could spend just five minutes leaving a review (it can be as short as you like) wherever you review books.

If you need a few tips on how best to write your review, *Huffington Post* has a quick checklist that can get you started.

Thank you very much.

Best regards,
Marion Hill

9 781734 644524